TEMPORARY GROOM

A Left At The Altar Novella

J.S. SCOTT

Temporary Groom

ISBN: 9781946660619 (ebook)

ISBN-13: 978-1719453806 (paperback)

Cover Design by Stacey Chappell

Formatting by Jera Publishing

STAY UP TO DATE AND FOLLOW ME ON:

Website: http://www.authorjsscott.com/

BookBub: https://www.bookbub.com/authors/j-s-scott

Instagram: https://www.instagram.com/authorj.s.scott/

Snapchat: https://www.snapchat.com/add/authorjsscott

Facebook: https://www.facebook.com/authorjsscott

Newsletter: http://bit.ly/1msPHkz

Twitter: https://twitter.com/AuthorJSScott

Goodreads: https://www.goodreads.com/author/show/277 7016.J_S_Scott

Pinterest: https://www.pinterest.com/jsscottauthor/

Amazon: http://www.amazon.com/J.S.-Scott/e/B007YUACRA/

CONTENTS

PROLOGUE

Lia

SEVEN YEARS AGO...

"*I* love you."

The words had just fallen out of my mouth. I hadn't stopped to think about them, nor was I worried about how my best friend, Zeke Conner, would interpret the statement.

In my more than slightly inebriated state, I just didn't care about anything.

And it had suddenly become of the utmost importance that Zeke knew how I really felt about him.

Maybe because I would have never said those words had I not been two sheets to the wind because it was my twenty-first birthday, and I'd spent the entire night getting drunk for the first time.

"I love you too, my little drunken friend," Zeke answered with a grunt as he hoisted me onto my bed.

Okay, maybe I needed to try again so he'd *really* understand what I meant. "I want to have sex with you," I confessed, my words sounding a little slurred. But he ought to get what I meant this time.

He grinned as he straightened up. "Everybody wants to have sex when they're drunk."

I frowned at him. Here I was, spilling my guts to him, and he wasn't taking me seriously.

It wasn't just the alcohol at work. Sure, I'd drunk *a lot*, and I wasn't in complete control of my words, but I really did love Zeke. I'd been crazy about him for years. But I'd never had the guts to admit it.

Now, I was ready to spill the fact that every wet dream I had revolved around him.

And he wasn't going to take me seriously.

"Where are you going?" I called to his retreating figure as I flopped back against my pillow.

"I'll be back," he hollered from the kitchen.

I tried to decide if the bed was really spinning as I listened to him rummage around in the kitchen.

My new apartment was tiny, but I loved it. I'd just moved out of my grandmother's house a few weeks ago because I'd gotten promoted to manager at the coffee shop I worked in.

Someday, I wanted to open my own place, but in the meantime, I was learning everything I could about the business of all things coffee.

I sighed as Zeke walked back into the room. He was so hot. And it wasn't easy having a best friend like him. Especially not when I wanted to be so much more than just his friend.

"Drink some water, and take these," he insisted as he sat on the bed and handed me a bottle of water. He put a few more bottles on the bedside table.

I held my hand out unsteadily, and he took it and tucked the aspirin into the palm of my hand.

I took the pills because he seemed to be waiting for me to do it, and then took some healthy slugs out of the water bottle he handed me.

"Drink water as long as you're awake. Lots of it. I'll be back in the morning with some food," he said gruffly.

Sometimes, Zeke could be a man of few words, but he got me. I was pretty sure he was the only person in the world who really did.

He'd spent the evening barhopping with me to celebrate my birthday, but he hadn't had more than one drink himself. As usual, he considered himself my protector, and it was his obligation to see me through my coming of age drinking spree.

He'd probably had better things to do than watch me get drunk, but it had been his idea to go on this mission while he was here on Thanksgiving break from college.

I sat up and carefully put the water down as I said, "Did you even hear me say I wanted to have sex with you?"

"I heard you," he said with humor in his tone. "But I know it's the alcohol talking."

"It's not," I argued, and wrapped my arms around his neck. "I really want it."

I felt his shoulders tense. We were suddenly face-to-face, so close that all I had to do was close the minimal distance between us and I'd finally have his mouth on mine.

I felt his warm breath on my face, and my body shuddered.

Wanting Zeke had become a habit I couldn't break, and a dream I couldn't seem to stop coveting.

His blue eyes turned stormy and turbulent as he stared at me. "It's not happening, Lia. I wanted to take you out to the bars so that I could watch out for you on your birthday. I don't want this, and neither do you. Being drunk makes everything look different. You won't feel the same way in the morning. Trust me."

I closed my eyes as he leaned forward and kissed my forehead, my disappointment flooding through me in waves.

I *wasn't* going to feel differently in the morning. I'd wanted my best friend for a long time, so I knew it was something that wasn't just going to go away.

He gently pulled my arms away from him and stood as he grumbled, "Call me if you need me."

I already needed him, but he'd just firmly and soundly pushed me away. "Okay," I answered, feeling dejected.

He didn't say another word as he exited the bedroom. I heard the apartment door open and close a few moments later.

I had no doubt he'd locked up since he had a key, and Zeke was nothing if not thorough in his desire to make sure I was safe.

I flopped back on the pillow again, regretting the abrupt motion because it made me dizzy.

My emotions were running rampant, and tears leaked from my eyes as I realized that I'd just been soundly rejected by the man I wanted most in the world.

He doesn't want me back.

I let out a strangled sob, and then another, until I finally cried myself to sleep.

The next morning, Zeke *did* come back as promised. I was hung over, but I felt better once I'd eaten breakfast.

Just like he'd warned, I was mortified that I'd confessed my feelings for him, and even more embarrassed because he'd firmly let me know he didn't feel the same way.

I think he assumed I didn't remember, and I certainly didn't bring it up.

Zeke and I were friends. Good friends. And the line I'd crossed the night before was horrifying.

I stuffed the adolescent emotions back inside me, so deep that I knew I'd never bring up the subject again. Hell, those feelings would never even see the light of day.

I had Zeke's friendship, and because he wanted nothing to do with a more intimate relationship, that was always going to have to be enough.

CHAPTER 1

Zeke

I'd never forgotten the first time I met Lia Harper, even though it was well over a decade ago. It was the first time I'd been the recipient of her gorgeous smiles that made me feel like her hero.

And I had no problem admitting that shit had become addictive over the years.

I'd been a senior in high school, and Lia had been a freshman.

Some bastard had been trying to feel her up in the hallway next to her locker.

And for some damn reason, I'd felt it was my duty to set the asshole straight about how fucking inappropriate it was to try to force himself on a female.

One broken nose—his, not mine—later, Lia had smiled at me, and my whole damn world had changed.

It hadn't been a sexual thing back then because that would just be creepy. But somehow I knew that nothing would ever be quite the same.

After I'd left her attacker on the hallway floor holding his bloody nose, I'd taken Lia home to her grandmother's house, and we'd been friends ever since.

The following year, I'd gone away to Harvard, but we'd seen each other on my college breaks, and in the summer. She'd been one of the best friends a guy could ask for, even when I was on the other side of the country attending the university.

Problem was, she'd grown up, and my dick had noticed it long before my brain had.

By the time I'd moved back to Seattle after I'd gotten my law degree, I'd already known I was royally screwed. I sure as hell had *wanted* to take our relationship to another level after college, but Lia hadn't seemed interested, and the last thing I wanted was to lose her as a friend.

Okay. Yeah. She'd once told me she wanted to have sex with me. Too bad she'd been too intoxicated at the time to know what she was saying. And she damn well hadn't mentioned it since, or I would have taken her up on the offer and gotten her naked before she could change her mind.

But after her twenty-first birthday, she'd treated me like I was her brother, making it pretty clear that she had no interest in exploring carnal knowledge of each other.

So I'd suffered in silence as I watched her date one guy after another, knowing damn well that not a single one of them was good enough for her. But don't feel too sorry for me. I became a man whore, hoping another woman would finally feel as right as Lia did when we were together.

Unfortunately, *that* had never happened.

There had been a time a year or two ago when I was ready to put our friendship on the line to tell her the truth. I'd psyched myself up to let her know that I thought we should be dating and burning up the sheets. But that was when she'd met Stuart, and I'd known I was completely fucked.

Her relationship with a guy I hated had turned into love, and then an engagement.

All those years of keeping my mouth shut was what brought me to my current predicament of sitting in a church, waiting for the woman I wanted to walk down the aisle to marry another man.

How could I *not* attend an event that was so important to Lia? That would make me a pretty shitty friend. And she didn't deserve that. It wasn't her fault that she'd never been attracted to me that way.

I looked around, noticing that the church was full. My gut already hurt, so I had no idea how I was going to manage watching Lia say her vows to the man she loved, a guy who wasn't...me.

Maybe if I thought she was going to be happy, this whole thing would be easier to swallow. Or...maybe not. I didn't know Stuart all that well, but enough to know he was a rich prick who wanted everything his way. We'd pretty much had a hate-hate relationship from our very first meeting at Lia's apartment.

It was the first time that jealousy had reared its ugly head inside me, and I'd never gotten past the feeling that Stuart was all wrong for Lia.

I squirmed on the uncomfortable bench seating, the necktie that matched my custom suit feeling like it was a little bit more snug than it had been when I'd put it on earlier, as I waited to hear the dreaded Wedding March.

I should have just fucking told her.

"Shit!" I cursed under my breath as I jerked on my tie. "I'm never going to be able to hold my peace."

There was no way I could be silent because I had plenty of *objections.* I just hadn't realized *quite how many* until I'd sat down in the church for the ceremony.

Maybe my timing wasn't exactly ideal, but I *knew* I couldn't let Lia marry Stuart without telling her exactly why she *shouldn't.*

I'd dropped plenty of hints, and Lia knew I thought Stuart was a jerk. But had I ever really told her that he wasn't ever going to be the guy she needed?

Nope.

I hadn't.

Not directly.

And I hated myself for it.

Stuart was never going to appreciate Lia for who she was. He'd try to mold her into somebody else who fit *his* ideal. He was already trying, and in the end, Lia would end up miserable.

Stuart would never understand her ambitions, and desire to make a difference in the world.

Stuart would never get Lia's addiction to Peanut M&M's.

The bastard would never comprehend why she cried at sad movies when someone died.

He'd never joke around or fight with her just to get her big-hearted hug when it was all over.

I felt a few droplets of sweat fall down my forehead as I stood up, my heart hammering against my chest wall.

It's not too late. Not yet. I can talk to her. Make her wait for somebody who will actually make her happy. Fuck Stuart.

As I made my way determinedly down the aisle, I knew that nothing would stop me from saying everything I'd never said.

Okay, maybe I *wouldn't* admit that she should be with me. That obviously wasn't something Lia had ever wanted, and I respected it. But I was going to finally lay out every single reason why she shouldn't be getting married to Stuart, minus my usual bullshit.

I was done being sarcastic about her choice, and throwing her hints about why I thought her fiancé was an asshole.

Reality had slapped me in the face a little bit late, but I was still reeling from the blow. And I wasn't going to be normal again until I talked to her.

Before the service started.

As I shoved my way through the closed double doors that lead to the hallway outside the chapel, I stopped abruptly when I lifted my gaze and saw Lia.

My *first thought* was how beautiful she looked in her wedding dress.

But after the initial quick glance, *the second thing* I noticed was the tears pouring down her face as she met my gaze.

She looked broken and upset.

So, *my last thought* as I pushed through the people around her, and she flung herself into my arms, was all about how I could make her happy again.

And *that* was the only thing that really mattered.

CHAPTER 2

Lia

*O**hmyGod! OhmyGod! OhmyGod! Stuart isn't here. He's not coming to the ceremony.*

My fiancé's brother had retreated as quickly as he'd arrived to give me the news that my husband-to-be had found a woman who was more suitable for him, and that Stuart was backing out of the wedding.

My entire body was trembling, and I could feel the tears of relief falling down my cheeks.

I'd woken up this morning with a sinking feeling in the pit of my stomach that I'd tried to ignore, but it wasn't until I'd pulled on my wedding dress in the changing room that I'd realized I couldn't get married.

Some strange force had finally knocked me in the head to get me thinking straight, and I'd been on my way to search out my fiancé when his brother had told me Stuart's news.

Granted, the bastard could have told me he was bailing out himself instead of sending his brother, but I was pretty sure I'd never been more at peace with a particular outcome than I was right now.

I pulled the stupid veil that Stuart's mother had insisted on from my head, and my eyes met a familiar stare as I looked over the heads of the small gathering around me.

Zeke. My friend. The one guy who had never let me down.

He was so tall and broad that he dwarfed almost everyone around him.

My best friend's startling blue-eyed gaze never left mine as he pushed his way through all of the people muttering their apologies. I found my reprieve by flinging myself into the arms of the one person who had always been there for me, sobbing out all my confusion on his muscular, powerful shoulder as his arms wrapped around me protectively.

"What happened?" Zeke's gentle voice queried as I settled down.

"Stuart is marrying somebody else," I said tearfully. "His brother just left. He only stopped by to let me know that Stuart had found a woman much better for him than me."

And I'm perfectly fine with it.

Granted, it doesn't feel good to get dumped, and it was humiliating to know that everybody would be talking about how Stuart had dumped the second-class woman he planned on marrying in favor of someone better. But those feelings were already fading away. Really, I'd just dodged a bullet. I was torn between wanting to punch Stuart and wanting to thank him for breaking things off, even though he'd done it in a pretty mortifying manner.

"Fuck!" Zeke cursed. "Let's get the hell out of here—unless you really want to stay."

I moved back and shook my head. "I can't. Not yet. I have to tell everybody—"

"I'll take care of it, Lia. Go with Zeke." I felt a gentle touch on my arm as the soft, female voice spoke.

My friend, Ruby, had obviously heard Zeke and me talking. "I can't just go."

"Yes, you can," she insisted. "And you will. You don't need to make the announcement yourself. Let Zeke get you out of here, and Jett and I will let everybody know."

"She's willing to handle it, Lia. Let her," Zeke insisted.

I bit my lip for a moment before I told Ruby, "Apparently, Stuart and his mother are taking care of the reception, returning the gifts, and all the rest of the stuff that has to be done."

Ruby snorted. "It's the least he can do."

I felt a painful twinge of guilt about the fact that Ruby had no idea that I wasn't completely a jilted bride. Had I talked to Stuart, I would have canceled the wedding myself. I just would have done it in a much nicer way than my now ex-fiancé had dumped me.

"Let's go," I said to Zeke.

I really needed to escape to get my head together.

Zeke grasped my hand and pulled me into the changing area so I could gather up my things.

We were outside the church and settling into his sleek, black Range Rover moments later.

"Where to?" he rumbled as he started the engine.

"It doesn't matter." I wanted to be anywhere but at the church.

"My place," he decided. "Nosy people will be a lot less likely to find you there."

It was doubtful that many people would really care, but Zeke was a wealthy man, and the security he had in his building was a lot better than mine.

"Okay," I agreed. His judgment was probably more sound than mine at the moment.

My brain was still trying to process the fact that the wedding I'd stressed over for the last year wasn't going to happen.

I never cared where I was with Zeke as long as we were together. It had always been that way.

I watched him rummage through the pockets of the suit jacket he'd taken off before he'd entered the vehicle, and I smiled when he finally found what he was looking for. He tossed the package into my lap.

"Thanks," I said gratefully as I picked up the small bag of Peanut M&M's and ripped them open.

I crunched on the candy as he drove, despite the fact that it wasn't helping me clear my mind. Maybe I wasn't as delighted as I usually was when Zeke tossed me my favorite indulgence, but it didn't hurt.

For me, chocolate was good for *any* occasion.

Our silence wasn't uncomfortable, and Zeke made a couple of quick stops on the way to his penthouse condo.

The two of us had been through a lot together, and sometimes silence was just fine.

I'd mourned and cried with him when he'd lost his father unexpectedly after he'd finished law school.

After that, he'd stayed with me during the paralyzing grief I'd gone through when my grandmother, who had been like a mother to me, had passed away.

For some strange reason, Zeke and I had always sensed what the other one needed. So I knew he was giving me my space, but physically being nearby if I needed him.

"I'm okay," I said with a sigh as we got close to his home.

"You just got dumped on your wedding day, Lia. I doubt very much that you're fine with that," Zeke answered in a hoarse voice.

Okay, maybe I felt like an idiot because I didn't call off the wedding sooner, but I certainly wasn't devastated. "He didn't love me. I made a lucky escape," I told him.

"I'm sure as hell not going to argue with you about that," he answered. "But he was a prick, Lia. You're definitely better off. But I know damn well that you're hurt. The bastard was obviously cheating on you."

I never lied to Zeke, but I couldn't bring myself to tell him that I was actually relieved, and that I'd been going to find my fiancé to break things off when I'd discovered that Stuart had wised up first.

Yeah, it grossed me out a little that Stuart had obviously slept with one or more females while we'd been in a committed relationship. But he always used a condom, and our sex life hadn't exactly been something I'd mourn. If I wanted to be totally honest, sleeping with him had been something I'd dreaded. However, I knew I'd be running to the clinic where I got my birth control to be tested for STDs come Monday morning.

The sadness I was feeling was more about being thrown away for a female who was better than me in the eyes of a man I was going to marry.

And when it came to disappointments, I was used to it. That was why I tried never to get too close to anybody.

Every time I loved somebody, they inevitably disappeared from my life.

The only person who had ever really reached past my defenses and stayed was Zeke.

My heart ached as I finally replied, "It doesn't matter, Zeke. I'll get over it."

It wouldn't be the first time a guy had found another woman who was far more responsive than I was in bed. I wasn't a female who really valued sex in her relationship all that much. In fact, one of my boyfriends had compared me to sleeping with a mannequin. And there was probably a little bit of truth to that, even though it had hurt at the time.

"Bullshit!" Zeke exploded. "Don't even try to tell me you're unaffected by this, Lia. I don't buy it. It's *me* you're talking to, and I know *you.* You can try to put on a brave face all you want, but you and I both know that deep inside, it hurts."

Yeah, my heart ached, and he could sense it. But it wasn't what he thought.

"Really, it doesn't," I confessed. "He didn't love me, Zeke, and I'm just starting to realize that I probably didn't love him. Maybe

I wanted the fantasy that every woman I know has found by now. Maybe I wanted to believe it would work for *me* this time. I'll be twenty-eight years old in a matter of days, and I guess I wanted the same kind of relationship most woman have had by my age. Stuart just wasn't the right one. Honestly, I'm not sure I let him get close enough to hurt me all that badly. He didn't demand anything beyond a façade, so that's probably why I thought it would be a good relationship. Neither one of us had to give much of ourselves."

Zeke pulled into his space at the parking garage, and slammed the vehicle into park before he turned to me. His eyes were the darker shade of blue that always appeared when he was really pissed off.

"You have a lot to offer any guy," he said gruffly. "You're beautiful, you're ambitious, you're wicked smart, and you're strong, Lia. Probably the toughest woman I've ever met. You should never settle for less than you deserve."

I swallowed the huge lump in my throat as I told Zeke something I'd never mentioned before. "I can't really get close to anybody. I've tried with every guy I've dated. But there's a wall inside me that just won't fall down. I'm too damn afraid to let it happen."

His face softened. "You're guarded. I know that. But it's not always a bad thing. You've been through way too much to let just anybody in."

I gathered up the ridiculous skirt of my gown and opened the passenger door as I replied, "I didn't let Stuart in. I couldn't. He wanted to change me. Make me into the woman he wanted to be married to, and I let him."

"I know," Zeke replied.

As I exited the SUV, I realized just how true my words were. I'd been so damn blinded by the fact that I wanted to share my life with someone that I'd allowed Stuart to take my power. I'd let him change me, make me into a woman I didn't even know anymore.

Zeke and I didn't speak as we rode the elevator up to his penthouse, but my mind was still racing.

Yeah, I was grateful that the wedding hadn't taken place. But I wondered how I was ever going to find myself again.

CHAPTER 3

Lia

One of Zeke's detours on the way home had been to pick up food from our favorite Chinese place. We were both foodies, but we hadn't shared a meal from our favorite spots in a long time.

I'd changed out of my dress and into a pair of jeans and a loose shirt, clothes that I'd left over at Zeke's place over time.

We both left some of the necessities at each other's homes, a habit we'd fallen into a long time ago for convenience.

The TV was on low in the background, but I was pretty sure neither one of us was paying attention to the news as we relaxed in Zeke's living room.

I finally dropped my fork on my plate and reached for the glass of white wine he'd poured me before he'd seated himself on the couch. I took a long sip before I said, "I don't know what I'm going to do about my grandma's will. If I'm not married by my birthday, I'm screwed."

I'd loved the grandparent who had raised me like her own after my parents had died in a car accident when I was twelve. Esther Harper, my father's mother, hadn't hesitated to move me from Michigan to Seattle to live with her, and we'd been close until she'd passed away two years earlier. But I still didn't get why she'd put the condition in her will that I couldn't inherit unless I was married by my twenty-eighth birthday. If I didn't, everything went to distant relatives we'd never even met, and charities she supported.

Not that Grandma Esther *owed* me anything. She'd raised me when nobody else would have taken me in. But it stung more than a little that she'd been trying to change me, too.

"I've looked at the documents," Zeke answered. "The estate attorney is right. If challenged, you could very well lose. It was written so well that it could be upheld by a judge."

Zeke's expression was grim, but I didn't doubt his opinion since my best friend was a high-powered defense attorney from a very powerful firm that he'd taken over when his father had died.

Even though he wasn't an expert at wills and trusts, Zeke was a Harvard Law graduate, and probably the smartest guy I knew.

So, that meant I had five days to get married or most likely forfeit my inheritance. While the funds weren't everything to me, I *had* borrowed six figures from Zeke to start my first coffee shop. Indulgent Brews had been so successful that I desperately wanted to start another one, and had planned on doing just that once the terms of the will were met.

"I'll have to up my installment payments to you," I said, feeling like a failure because I couldn't pay off the money I owed to him. "I don't know how else to get you paid back. And the second Indulgent Brews will have to wait."

"I don't need the money," Zeke answered grumpily. "And I'm your silent partner."

The argument was a familiar one. We'd had it nearly every time we talked. "You didn't want to be a partner," I reminded him. "You did it to help me."

He was right. He *didn't* need the money. Zeke Conner came from a wealthy family, and at the age of thirty-two, was the head of one of the most successful law firms in Seattle.

"Knowing you don't need it doesn't make me feel that much better about the fact that I can't pay you back. You're my friend, Zeke," I said remorsefully.

"If you feel that bad, you could just marry me," he answered matter-of-factly.

I started to laugh, but then halted abruptly as I looked at him on the couch from my place in a recliner.

He was staring at me with a look I knew. An expression that had none of his usual humor or teasing.

Holy shit! He's serious.

I set my empty wine glass on the side table and folded my arms in front of me. "I'm pretty sure Angelique wouldn't be happy," I said in an easy tone.

He shrugged his massive shoulders. "We broke up, not that we were ever really a couple in the first place. But I haven't seen her in months. Where have you been?"

Where have I been?

I'd been so busy trying to hire a new manager for my shop, and preparing for my wedding, that I'd obviously failed to notice that Zeke didn't have the gorgeous brunette on his arm anymore.

"I'm sorry," I answered, feeling like a shit because I hadn't known that Zeke was flying solo.

"Don't be. It was never serious."

I sighed as I leaned back into the comfortable chair. "Who broke it off?" I asked curiously.

"Mutual agreement," he replied.

God, I hated the fact that no woman had ever really looked past Zeke's eligibility and his money. Sure, women found him attractive. Who wouldn't?

It had *never* escaped my notice that Zeke was hot. It still didn't. I'd just tried to ignore it for the good of our friendship after I'd spilled my guts to him on my twenty-first birthday and had gotten rejected.

I stared at him blatantly, taking in his powerful, ripped body, the sandy-colored blondish-brown hair, and his beautiful blue eyes with lashes that I'd always envied before I said, "Your relationships are never serious. Don't you want to get married eventually?"

Strangely, I felt more than one twinge of uneasiness at the thought of Zeke pledging his life to a woman. I'd never really contemplated that before, maybe because he'd never seemed to get serious with any woman in particular. But just the thought of losing him to a woman who wouldn't tolerate him being friends with a female was unnerving.

Stuart had tried to bully me into giving up my friendship with Zeke, but it was one thing I'd stood strong on. Zeke was my friend and always would be as far as I was concerned. However, I had no idea what would happen in the future with *him.*

He looked up and pinned my gaze with his. "I think I just offered to marry you. Does that mean you're refusing?"

The timbre of his voice sent an electric zing down my spine. I wasn't immune to the dangerous, wickedly low tone of his voice. I just wanted to think it didn't make every female hormone in my body stand up and take notice. "You weren't serious."

"I was completely serious, Lia. You need to get married. I'm available."

Oh, *sweet Jesus,* I *knew* that intense expression. I just hadn't seen it in a very long time. "You can't just marry me," I protested. "I adore you for offering, but that's just crazy."

Problem was, I knew Ezekiel Conner was far from insane.

He was funny.

He could be sweet when he wanted to be.

He oozed a masculine sex appeal that most women couldn't ignore.

He was incredibly wealthy.

He was smart, successful, and every woman's dream.

But he was my friend.

Women like me did not marry men like Zeke Conner.

He was way too...perfect.

"Think about it, Lia. You deserve to open another store, and to get out from under the expenses you acquired from the first one. You don't want to accept the money I gave you as a gift, so that means you feel like you have to pay it back before you can keep moving forward. If you marry me, you don't have to commit to forever. There's nothing in the will that requires you to stay married. You meet the terms, collect your inheritance, and then get a divorce if that's what you want."

I gaped at him. "I don't get it. What do you get from this?" I chewed on a fingernail nervously as my eyes stayed fixed on his.

"Do you really want to know?" he asked huskily.

I nodded slowly.

"I get *you* in my bed for as long as it takes to get your inheritance," he answered with what sounded like a bluntly honest tone.

"Why would you want *that*?" I squeaked.

I'd offered myself up to him once, and I'd regretted it ever since.

Zeke had been my friend for fourteen years, and there had never been a single mention of anything more than friendship between the two of us except for my drunken confession on my twenty-first birthday.

"Did you really think that I haven't noticed that you grew into a beautiful woman?"

"You've never wanted to screw me," I challenged.

"Sure I did," he said with a smirk. "What red-blooded man wouldn't?"

"Tons of them," I said nervously.

All of my ex-boyfriends, at least.

"I do want to fuck you," he said as he folded his muscular arms across his chest. "I've just never mentioned it. You were engaged, and unlike your asshole ex-fiancé, I knew you'd never cheat on a man."

His expression was stoic, and for the first time in our long friendship, I had absolutely no idea what he was thinking.

This man wasn't the Zeke I knew, but he was still familiar. I felt like I was in some kind of weird dream, and seeing a side of him that I'd never noticed before.

But he's still my Zeke.

I *did* start thinking about his offer because he'd asked me to do it. Maybe his hadn't been the most romantic proposal in the world, but the fact that he'd sacrifice his freedom, even temporarily, for me made my eyes well up with tears.

Not that I was buying the crap about him lusting after my body. It was his way of pretending he'd get something out of the deal if I said yes.

But I wanted to pay him back for everything he'd done since I'd opened my successful coffee shop. And the only way I was going to be able to do that was to get my inheritance.

He'd trusted me, and I wanted to be worthy of the faith he'd always had in me.

Not only had Zeke given me the money generously, but he'd been there for me every step of the way. He called himself a silent partner, but he'd been around when shit hit the fan, too. Zeke even worked the store during rush hours when I was overwhelmed.

This man had always been there to help me. Now, I wanted to show him that I was able to thrive because he'd had faith in me.

"Okay," I said, my decision made.

He lifted a brow. "Okay...what?"

"I'll marry you. But don't think for a single second that I believe that you want my body. But I'll make sure your sacrifice is worth it to you somehow."

"But you agree to the terms?" he asked.

I snorted. "Yeah. Okay. I agree."

I was okay with keeping up the pretense that he was lusting after me if he wanted to. But I knew he was doing me a favor—again.

He grinned at me, a mischievous smile I hadn't seen from him in a long time. "Then I'll make damn sure it's worth it to you, too."

My heart tripped, his sexy baritone affecting me in a way it never had before.

This is all temporary. Don't start thinking it's anything more than a friend helping a friend in a pretty profound way.

I smiled back at him because I couldn't help myself, but inside I kept reminding myself that the agreement wasn't going to last forever.

I had no idea why the thought that Zeke was just pretending to be attracted to me made me slightly sad.

CHAPTER 4

"*S*he didn't believe me when I said I wanted her," I muttered unhappily to my friend, billionaire tech mogul, Jett Lawson.

Jett's fiancée, Ruby, had left his penthouse with Lia. The moment Lia had told Ruby that she needed to plan a second wedding in a hurry, the two of them had hightailed it out of the building to go arrange the event.

Ruby had met Lia first, and in addition to being friends, the two women saw each other almost every day since Ruby supplied the baked goods for Lia's coffee shop, Indulgent Brews.

In spite of the fact that Jett Lawson was one of the richest men in the world, he was a nice guy, and we'd become friends, too.

Hell, maybe misery did love company. Jett was trying to give Ruby some time and space before their wedding took place because Ruby was only twenty-three, and she'd been through hell. But I knew it was killing him to wait.

"Then you'll have to seduce her," Jett answered. "Where is the honeymoon?"

"I haven't really thought about that," I said, annoyed with myself that the honeymoon had never entered my mind.

I'd been too damn focused on the fact that Lia was going to be mine. To hell with the "temporary" shit. I had to find a way to convince her that we belonged together.

"She trained up a manager for the store, and Ruby is there almost every day. We can watch the shop."

Lia had only gotten a manager because she had planned on being on her honeymoon with Stuart. I grimaced as I informed him, "Stuart was taking her to Dubai."

"On their honeymoon?" Jett questioned, his face incredulous. "She'd have to dress conservatively. No touching in public, either. What in the hell was he thinking? That's not a romantic honeymoon."

"He apparently has some business interests there, and wants to drum up a few more," I grumbled.

"Asshole," Jett said irritably.

I nodded. "Definitely."

"You need to take her someplace warm and romantic. Hell, I'm no expert on women, but there are a lot more romantic places in the world to go," Jett suggested.

"Bora Bora?" I considered aloud.

Jett shook his head. "Too far into fall. You'll hit the rainy season."

I shrugged. "So we'll end up shacked up together in an over-water bungalow."

There was nobody I'd rather be rained-in with than Lia.

"Stop thinking with your dick," Jett insisted. "You can't have sex every minute of your honeymoon."

Considering how long I'd wanted Lia, I was pretty sure I could spend the entire time getting naked with her, but Jett was right. No matter how much I wanted to fuck her, I also wanted to see her smile. I probably wanted her to be happy more than I wanted to get her naked, and that was saying something.

"Hawaii?"

Jett shook his head. "Uninspired. Everybody goes there."

"Bahamas?"

"Boring," he replied.

"Cancun," I growled, getting annoyed.

"I'd go for Playa del Carmen," he countered.

I'd been to both Cancun and Playa. They were close to each other, but Jett was right. Playa was a little quieter, but didn't lack for things to do.

"I'll get the trip planned," I agreed.

"She'll love it," Jett replied, like he hadn't just told me that I was uninspired.

Hell, I was plenty *inspired.* I'd be on my honeymoon with the woman who had haunted my wet dreams for years.

"I want this trip to be special for her," I shared. "Lia has never really traveled, and I know she wants to. I should have offered to take her on vacation a long time ago, but I guess it just never came up."

Jett lifted a brow. "You were never planning to sleep in the same room before."

I shrugged. "Still, she's my friend, the best one I've got."

"Ruby is my best friend," Jett considered. "But that doesn't mean I don't want to touch her every time I see her. Honestly, I have no idea how you've managed to keep your hands off Lia if you have the same feelings for her that I do for Ruby."

I heaved a sigh as I reached for the beer Jett had given me a little earlier. "I guess I didn't always feel this way. Lia was fourteen when we met, too damn young for a guy who was almost eighteen. All I really wanted back then was to protect her."

"But that changed when?" Jett questioned.

"I guess it was while I was going to college. But she was still pretty damn young, so I tried to tell myself that I was just in my sexual prime, and it would go away."

"It didn't," Jett concluded.

"Hell, no. It just got worse." I chugged some of my beer before I added, "But the timing was never right. One or both of us was always seeing somebody else."

"You would have let her marry another guy?" Jett reached for his own drink as he sat across from me on the couch.

"No. I couldn't. I guess I just snapped yesterday. I was on my way to tell her every reason why I didn't think she should marry Stuart, but the bastard's brother had already found Lia to call off the wedding because Stuart had met somebody else."

"Ouch," Jett said sympathetically. "Ruby told me what happened, and that's pretty damn cold."

"Exactly," I agreed. "Can you imagine being dumped like that? And what in the hell was he thinking? Lia is the very best he could ever have, and the dumbass never even appreciated her."

"I have a feeling you won't make the same mistake," Jett said drily.

I put my empty beer bottle on the side table. "I wouldn't," I confirmed. "But Lia isn't taking any of this seriously. She thinks I'm doing some kind of noble sacrifice to help her get her inheritance."

Jett nodded slowly. "Yeah, Ruby told me about the will requirements. It's kind of strange. Was her grandmother in her right mind when she did it?"

I let out a bark of laughter. "You didn't know Esther," I informed him. "She was as sharp as a tack until the day she died. I don't completely get it, either. She adored her granddaughter, and Lia took care of Esther when she was sick. I don't understand why she made *any* rules for the inheritance. And there's nothing that says that Lia has to stay married for any length of time. She just wanted her...married. Not like Esther at all."

"So the terms are easy to fulfill?"

"Very," I informed him. "Lia asked me to look over every document, and I have. I'm not an expert in wills and trusts, but it was pretty straightforward."

"Do you think Lia was convinced that she had to marry Stuart because of the money?"

I frowned at Jett. "No. She had plenty of time to back out. And she didn't exactly give a damn about the money other than the fact that she couldn't pay me back. I think she convinced herself that she loved him, and that he was her perfect partner. I have no fucking idea why."

"Is she okay?" he asked in a serious tone. "I mean, she didn't really look terribly broken up earlier, but it could all be an act."

"She'll be fine," I said. "I'll make sure that she is."

"You need to tell her how you feel," Jett insisted. "Keeping your mouth shut hasn't gotten you anywhere."

"I tried. Like I said, she thinks I'm just making up a reason to help her."

Jett rose from the couch and I followed him into the kitchen. I gratefully took the second bottle of beer from him as we both leaned against the counter.

He took a gulp from his own chilly bottle before he said, "Make her listen. Maybe *you* haven't confronted how you felt until yesterday. But it's pretty damn obvious that you care about her."

I nodded, giving up all pretense. "I have for a long time. I can't exactly pinpoint the moment that everything changed for me. Hell, I've been in major denial because I knew she was going to marry somebody else. But I'm over worrying about whether or not I'm going to lose Lia completely if I tell her."

Lia Harper and I were never meant to be just friends. Not once we'd both become adults. Not in my mind, anyway. And ever since I'd really come to terms with the fact that I had to risk everything to get what I wanted, I'd been okay with that.

"At least you'll be able to say you tried," Jett agreed.

"Failure really is not an option," I said gruffly.

"Then don't fail," he suggested.

"I don't plan on it," I confirmed in a tone that was almost a growl.

Lia didn't know it yet, but she *was* going to be mine.

And I didn't mind playing *dirty* to make sure it happened. In fact, I relished getting just as dirty as we could get.

CHAPTER 5

Lia

"What in the hell am I doing?" I asked my friend, Ruby, in a moment of panic.

Only a few days ago, I'd been getting ready for my wedding to Stuart, and now I was just about ready to walk down the aisle with my best friend.

I had no idea how we'd managed to pull this whole thing together, but I'd forever be grateful to Ruby, and to Zeke's mother, Marlene.

Zeke's mom had been elated when she learned that her son and I were getting married, and she'd taken the whole last-minute wedding thing in stride. If I didn't already think she was an amazing woman—which I did—I'd be totally in awe of her skills.

Marlene had hooked up with Ruby and me by video chat, and arranged to get us hitched in a century-old chapel in Gig Harbor, a lovely town about an hour from Seattle in good traffic. And the reception was taking place at the yacht club nearby.

Everything had come together perfectly, but the fact that I was actually marrying Zeke was still surreal.

"You're getting married to the right man this time," Ruby answered as she smoothed down the skirt of my second wedding dress. "And you look gorgeous."

I had to admit that I felt pretty as I looked at my reflection in the mirror.

I'd had no qualms about trading in the dress I'd had for my wedding to Stuart since I'd paid for the dress I'd never liked in the first place.

The traditional dress with the long train and old-fashioned veil had never been my style. So I'd opted for something I could feel comfortable in.

"It's a really nice dress," I said as I looked at the deceptively simple long-sleeved ivory gown. There was no veil, no train. My current choice was a vintage style that cinched at the waist, and fell in curtains of silk and lace to my feet.

When I caught Ruby's reflection in the mirror as she flitted around to arrange my dress, I added, "You look gorgeous, too."

Ruby stood up straight next to me in her muted dusty-rose silk gown. "I feel like a princess," she said breathlessly. "I've never had a dress this beautiful."

I shot her a tremulous smile. Ruby had been homeless before she'd met Jett. So I loved seeing a smile on her face over a simple bridesmaid dress. Actually, it was humbling.

Oh, God. I really hoped I was doing the right thing. "I just feel so guilty," I confessed. "You know this is all a ruse, but Marlene doesn't. And she's so happy."

"Does it feel right?" Ruby asked as she fussed with the silver clips that were holding my curly blonde hair back from my face.

"Strangely, it doesn't feel wrong," I told her. "I know that sounds weird, but I trust Zeke. I always have."

"Then roll with it," Ruby replied. "And stop feeling guilty. Zeke really wants this, and I think you do, too. I know you think this isn't real, but there's a marriage license that says differently. I think you'll both be happy."

"You're saying that like I'm staying married," I answered.

Ruby shrugged. "Who says you won't? Maybe you'll come back from your honeymoon knowing that Zeke is the right guy for you. I think he always has been, but you just never noticed."

"Zeke and me?" I squeaked. "That's crazy. We've always been just friends. Guys like Zeke don't marry women like me."

Ruby gave me a disbelieving look. "Why wouldn't they?"

"He's rich, and he's obscenely hot. Zeke is educated, a Harvard Law graduate. He's in control of one of the most prestigious law firms in the city. I'm not even remotely the woman for someone like him."

Ruby pulled a face. "Please. Don't start talking about a guy being out of your league. I'm a homeless woman who just got engaged to one of the richest men in the world. Sometimes those superficial things just don't matter. It's what's in here that counts." She thumped a hand on her chest.

She was right. "But we've always been friends."

Ruby rolled her eyes. "Not for Zeke. He's always looked at you like you were the only female who existed. If he looked at you as a friend, it was a long time ago. The guy adores you. It's pretty obvious. Are you saying that you've never seen him as an attractive guy?"

"I did. I do. I just never thought about...him being mine. I admit, I was infatuated with him when I was younger, but even then, I wasn't thinking he'd ever marry me."

Ruby let out a playful laugh. "Well, you better consider it, because you're about to walk down the aisle, and your groom looks a lot like Zeke."

"But you know it's not for real." Zeke was doing all of this for me, and I shuddered as I thought about just how much he was giving up to do this whole charade.

"We'll see. You've obviously never seen the way he looks at you," Ruby answered mysteriously as she took my hand and led me the short distance to the chapel.

The distance from the doorway to the altar wasn't exactly long, and Ruby managed to get there faster than I could blink.

I froze. As I looked around the small venue at the family and friends who had come to see Zeke and me get married, I realized the gravity of my decision.

Oh God, I can't do this to my best friend.

I know he cares about me, but I can't make him marry me just to get my inheritance.

I have to stop this right now.

It was like déjà vu. Except I wouldn't be calling the wedding off for *me* this time. I'd be doing it for *Zeke.*

I'd gotten so caught up in doing tasks that had to be done over the last few days that I'd failed to think about how *really* unfair this all was to Zeke. Maybe because he kept telling me that it was no big deal.

But it was a *very big deal.*

I looked up, and I met Zeke's beautiful eyes across the small room. His gaze was steady and reassuring, but I couldn't shake the guilt that was pummeling me.

I didn't move, so he stepped down from the platform and made his way to my side.

"You're not backing out," he said roughly in my ear as he took my hand. "Don't even think about it."

I wasn't surprised that he knew exactly what I was thinking. He usually did.

"I'm sorry. I can't do this," I whispered loud enough so that he could hear. "It's just not right. I should have never said yes."

"We're going to walk down this aisle together. Come on, Lia. We've always made it through everything together. And this is no different. Walk with me. You look stunningly gorgeous, and my family is here. Please don't make me tell them that the wedding isn't happening."

I didn't have any relatives in the small gathering, but Zeke had family present. A few cousins, an aunt, an uncle, and most importantly, his mother.

I felt my heart galloping in my chest as I tilted my head and looked up at him. "This can't be what you really want," I said breathlessly. "Even if it's only temporary."

He pinned me with an intense stare that I'd never experienced before. "You're wrong. I do want this."

"I don't understand," I said, feeling confused.

"You will," he answered ominously. "Just marry me."

The last thing I wanted was to embarrass him, so I squeezed his hand. "Never say I didn't give you an out."

Like I'd told Ruby, I trusted Zeke. I wasn't afraid of the consequences. But I was concerned about the fallout for him.

"I don't need an out, Lia," he answered.

I nodded slowly. "Okay."

It was hard to take my eyes off him as I moved into position to walk beside him. I'd never seen Zeke in a tuxedo, and it looked pretty damn good on him.

"Smile," he insisted as we walked toward the altar.

I felt twice as guilty as I saw Marlene in the front row, grinning from ear to ear. She winked, and I kept smiling as I passed her and we stopped in front of the man officiating the ceremony.

Ruby and Jett had agreed to stand up for us, and Ruby reached out to take my flowers as I turned to Zeke.

Somewhere between the beginning of the ceremony and the end, everything started to feel real to me.

The sincere timbre of Zeke's voice as he took his vows, and the way he promised so steadfastly to love and honor me, made all of this feel real. Just like the words I said that bound me to him had come naturally.

Zeke had handled the rings, and I let out an audible gasp as he slipped a gorgeous diamond on my finger. It was huge, and a vintage style I would have chosen for myself.

And then, he kissed me.

It felt so much like he was staking his claim.

It was an embrace that felt like a promise.

And as I wrapped my arms around his neck and kissed him back, I knew nothing would be the same between us ever again.

CHAPTER 6

Lia

"This is amazing," I said with a moan right after I'd swallowed the first bite of the wedding cake we'd just finished cutting.

Zeke had taken care of the cake, too, and I'd nearly started to bawl when I saw that it was a blueberry lemon cake. I loved blueberry. I was a Michigan girl, after all. But I was touched that he'd remembered, and ordered a cake he knew I'd love.

Honestly, it felt strange for a guy to give a damn what I wanted. Stuart had gotten what was trendy, and he hadn't consulted me much about anything since he'd been paying for our wedding. A fact he'd reminded me about every single time I made a suggestion. I'd finally just...given up on anything I wanted.

Our reception consisted of one very large table of guests, but for me, it was perfect.

I'd never wanted the large, formal, uptight wedding Stuart had planned. If I had been able to choose, it would have been just like this. Friends and family instead of worrying about what business people he had to impress.

In my opinion, weddings were very personal, and should be about the couple instead of the people in attendance.

"Thank you for getting my favorite," I whispered beside Zeke's ear as I leaned into him so nobody else could hear me.

I'd gotten so close that I could smell him, which probably wasn't a good thing. His masculine scent and the proximity of our bodies was a very heady thing. After the kiss he'd laid on me at the end of the wedding ceremony, my entire body had come to life. To be honest, I was still reeling over the embrace. For a few moments, I'd been so intoxicated by the feel of his soft lips on mine that I'd forgotten anybody was in the chapel except him.

We'd eaten an incredible catered meal, and we were now back in our seats at the table, devouring a huge piece of wedding cake.

"I have to admit that I debated between the M&M and blueberry cakes, but of course I was going to get one of them. It's your wedding and you like both of them."

I practically melted into a pool under the table. Zeke acted like there was no other option except something I liked, which was a novel experience for me. Like it was important to please me. Funny how that seemed so romantic after my previous experience.

"This is perfect," I informed him as I pointed my fork at the nearly demolished cake on my plate.

"Did I tell you how beautiful you look today?" he asked huskily.

"You did," I assured him. And he had...at least ten times since he'd seen me at the chapel. "Do you like the dress?"

"Love it," he replied enthusiastically.

"You look hot in a tux," I told him as I scooped the last piece of cake into my mouth.

He turned to look at me. "You noticed," he teased.

I rolled my eyes. "You might be my friend, but I'm not blind."

"Do you want to tell me what happened before the ceremony? You looked terrified, and I was pretty sure you were ready to bolt. I didn't realize you found marrying me that damn daunting."

I dropped my fork on my empty plate and then looked at the rest of the table. The guests were way too involved in the food to be listening. "It wasn't like that. I guess I just realized how one-sided this deal is for you. I'll get my inheritance at the price of your freedom, even if it's only temporary."

"Do I look worried?" he asked lightly.

"No. And that kind of scares the hell out of me," I confessed. "You wouldn't even do a pre-nuptial agreement. I appreciate the fact that you trust me, but you have a lot more to lose than I do. I'm actually gaining with this whole thing. You aren't."

"Kiss! Kiss! Kiss!"

To my chagrin, the whole table was clinking their forks against their glasses, insisting that Zeke and I share an embrace.

He put a finger under my chin and tipped my head up as he grumbled, "I'm not getting nothing, Lia. I'm getting you."

I shivered as his lips met mine in an even more intimate embrace than we'd shared at the altar. This one was a lazy, thorough exploration that made me breathless, and I couldn't stop myself from kissing him back.

He devoured, and I opened for him to get him closer, my body responding like a fireworks show on the Fourth of July. Zeke filled every one of my senses, and I lost myself in his insistent, sensual assault.

Granted, it was a little strange to suddenly want to rip my best friend's clothes from his body so I could intimately explore every powerful muscle and every inch of his bare skin. But somehow, it also felt as natural as breathing. And as important as oxygen.

A longing I'd never experienced gripped me, and it refused to let go.

"Zeke," I whispered as though I was in a daze as he finally released my mouth.

"Don't be afraid, Lia. Just let it happen," he said hoarsely.

"But we're friends. None of this is real," I answered shakily, realizing I was having trouble separating reality from fantasy because of my reaction when I was close to Zeke.

"Right now, we're married. I think we're a hell of a lot more than friends."

"Hey, get a room," one of Zeke's young cousins shouted from the other end of the table.

He grinned. "I plan on it," Zeke called back.

The moment of intimacy was broken, but I couldn't stop thinking about what he'd said.

Let it happen.

Really, did I have any choice when Zeke kissed me like he just had? I was pretty much defenseless when he started a powerful sensual assault.

"We should be able to make our escape pretty soon," Zeke said.

We'd decided that it was best if we lived at Zeke's place, and most of my clothing had already been sent there.

I nodded. "Back to your place."

"We aren't going home. I packed some of your things, and they're in the car. We have to leave from here to the airport. There's a charter waiting."

I was dumbfounded. "Why are we going to the airport?"

He shot me a brilliant grin. "We just got married. We're going on our honeymoon."

I frowned. The last thing I wanted was a honeymoon. Stuart had arranged a trip to Dubai, and I had been planning on suffering through it. So I was more than happy to just hang out at Zeke's place. "Where?"

"Playa del Carmen," he answered. "Maybe I should have asked you, but I thought you'd love to go someplace tropical and relaxing after the stress you've been through."

I'd never been to Playa, but I knew it was close to Cancun on the Yucatan Peninsula, and since it was gloomy and rainy in Seattle, it sounded like heaven.

I sighed. "I'd love to go somewhere like that."

"We are going," he replied.

"But my shop—"

"Will be just fine," he interrupted. "You have a manager, and Ruby will check in every day. We can do as much or as little as you want there. Snorkel, boat rides in the underground caves, the pool, the fantastic beaches, zip-lining, exploring the Mayan ruins, and eating at all the best restaurants we can find."

I laughed. "You don't exactly have to twist my arm to spend time in the Caribbean."

Luckily, I'd had to get a passport for my impending honeymoon with Stuart. But Zeke's sounded like a hell of a lot more fun and relaxing.

I'd never had a real vacation, and I'd always dreamed of getting to Mexico.

"Good. Then we're off just as soon as we can flee," he said with a hint of mischief in his tone.

I noticed that the music had started, but nobody had gotten out of their seat yet.

"Nobody is dancing," I told him.

"They're waiting for us," he explained as he got to his feet. "Dance with me, Mrs. Conner?"

Zeke held out his hand.

My heart skittered as I looked up and saw him looking at me expectantly.

I wasn't entirely sure that our bodies being wrapped together was a very good idea. But I decided to throw caution to the wind.

I took his hand and stood up.

Just let it happen.

He'd been so confident, so sure that letting go of everything and just enjoying the experience was the right thing to do.

But I knew I wasn't going to be doing that just because Zeke thought it was the right thing to do.

As I followed him to the small dance floor, I knew I was making the decision because I wanted to.

CHAPTER 7

Lia

The following day, I was basking in the sun and warmth of the gorgeous beach in Playa, wondering what I did to deserve such a fantastic honeymoon.

Zeke had put us in a swanky resort suite with two bedrooms, and the luxurious resort had every available amenity.

Since we'd gotten in late last night, we'd both retreated to our rooms, and then slept late this morning.

God, I couldn't remember a time when I'd been allowed to sleep until mid-morning. And if that had ever happened, I certainly hadn't thrown on a swimsuit and headed to the beach when I'd woken up.

I turned my head to look at Zeke, who was in the lounger next to mine, my eyes fixed on the simple platinum band I'd put on his finger the day before. It winked brightly in the sun, and my belly clenched. *Hard.*

For some reason, I still couldn't quite fathom Zeke as my husband, even if it was only going to last for a little while. Now that the craziness was over, I couldn't seem to stop thinking about it...or him.

Maybe it was the fact that neither one of us was heavily clothed. Zeke was in a pair of board shorts, his perfectly formed body on full display.

To put it simply, my new husband had the body of a god. My eyes roamed over every inch of his muscular chest, and I itched to touch the smooth skin that covered his six-pack abs.

Tearing my eyes away, I reached for the fruity drink on the small table between us, trying to find some relief from the gnawing ache between my thighs.

"It's beautiful here," I said after I'd guzzled a large portion of my drink.

The beach was private, and only used by the resort. So it was far from crowded. Zeke and I had our own little portion of it, even if there were other guests around.

"Are you thawed out yet?" he asked in a teasing voice.

"Almost." Seattle had been cool and rainy, so I pretty much felt like I was in paradise. "Thank you for this. I think I needed it."

"I think we both did," he agreed. "Honestly, it's been a long time since I've gotten away from Seattle."

Zeke worked so hard that I couldn't remember the last time he'd escaped, either. Sadly, I also couldn't recollect the last time he'd really laughed and had fun. We'd both been so caught up in our lives that I suddenly realized that in some respects, we'd drifted apart.

Yeah, we saw each other a lot at the coffee shop because he stopped in often. But when had we quit going out together, having fun together?

Thinking back, I guess it had all been different since Stuart and I had started dating.

"I've missed you," I said before I could censor my words.

"I missed you, too, Lia. A lot," he said in a graveled voice.

"How did we start drifting apart?"

"When you decided Stuart was the best thing that ever happened to you," he drawled. "I knew he wasn't, and I couldn't stand to watch him try to change you. You were perfect just the way you were."

"Did I change?" I asked curiously, knowing full well that I had.

"Yes. Stuart somehow managed to dim the bright light you always seemed to carry around inside you. And you were never meant to be subdued." He shot me a smile, but his expressive eyes were covered with a pair of dark sunglasses.

I leaned my head back against the lounge pillow and closed my eyes. "I'm not even sure how or when it happened," I admitted. "Little by little, I just gave up disagreeing with him about everything from my clothing to my hair style. It was just easier. And he made me second-guess myself."

"Why?" Zeke asked. "At one time, you'd tell the entire world to go screw themselves if they didn't like you."

I shrugged. "He knew how to manipulate my insecurities. I got to the point where I felt like being me wasn't good enough."

"He was so fucking wrong," Zeke growled. "You know that, right? Nobody should ever want you to change in order to get their love and acceptance."

"I know," I replied. "But that's easier to see when the relationship is over than when it's happening. I guess I never really wanted to acknowledge that I was doing all the compromising."

In short, Stuart was an asshole. He'd criticized me every single day, and I let myself absorb every fault he pointed out until I was a different version of myself. A Lia I really hadn't liked.

He'd been in control.

And I'd merely been an observer.

I felt so damn lost that I wasn't sure I was ever going to find myself again. Not that I actually missed *him*, but because I'd let him call the shots for so long and dictate who I was as a person.

My eyes flew open as I felt Zeke put his hand over mine. "Everything will be okay, Lia."

For some reason, I desperately wanted to cry. "You tried to tell me, but I wasn't listening."

"I didn't try hard enough," he said roughly. "Let's go cool off. You ready to go for a swim?"

I was beyond ready. "Do you want to go to the pool?"

He stood and pulled me up gently beside him. "Hell, no. The sea temperature has to be over eighty-five degrees."

I glanced at the beautiful turquoise water before I lifted the cover-up I was wearing over my head, and tossed it in the chair. I'd only had one simple, black, one-piece swimming suit, so that was what I was wearing beneath it.

My body filled with anticipation as I bolted toward the Caribbean, kicking up some of the gorgeous white sand as I called, "I'll get there first."

Zeke didn't catch up to me until I was in the water.

It was warm, but the shock of hitting the ocean waters and Zeke wrapping his arms around me from behind made me squeal.

"Cheater," he accused.

I was in waist-deep water as I turned around and laughed. "All I did was run. You're just getting slow."

"You distracted me," he said as he grinned down at me, his chest and face already wet from the initial splash we'd made when we'd plowed into the ocean waters. "A guy can't possibly *not* be distracted when your beautiful ass is headed toward the water."

He hauled me against him, and I trembled as he wrapped his powerful arms around my waist.

He felt so good. So warm. So damned...tempting.

Time stopped as his liquid blue eyes pinned mine as though he was searching for something. My heart kicked against my chest wall.

"Zeke," I said breathlessly, not knowing what to say about the way he made me feel.

He was so close that I could feel his warm breath against my lips.

"You're so fucking beautiful, Lia," he rasped right before his mouth covered mine.

My body caught fire, and I wrapped my arms around his neck, savoring every brush of my fingers against his bare skin.

Carnal desire flooded my senses, and I couldn't get enough of his marauding mouth, so I pushed back, meeting every stroke of his tongue.

And it felt so perfect, so natural that I wasn't afraid to let him in.

The way that Zeke consumed me felt so right that I couldn't imagine it being wrong.

He was different, yet familiar at the same time. And I couldn't get enough.

Water was lapping lovingly against my body, but all I could really feel was Zeke.

I clung to him like a second skin. And I didn't want to ever let go. He touched me like I was the most necessary thing in the world to him.

It was addictive.

Seductive.

And completely all-consuming.

I was panting when he finally released my mouth, his lips trailing to the sensitive skin of my neck, leaving a trail of fire in his wake as he said, "I want you so damn much, Lia."

Incredibly, I wanted him, too. More than I could express in words, but I tried. "I don't understand this. We're supposed to be friends."

"Let it happen," he said roughly against my neck. "Don't second-guess the way we feel together."

Since I'd never been a very sexual female, it was hard to just give in. I wasn't sure why I felt like I had to figure it out when I knew Zeke was right. I could just let myself feel, because what I was experiencing was very, very real.

My core clenched painfully as Zeke's mouth brushed against my ear. My body was demanding satisfaction. And dammit,

I wanted to climb up his muscular body until I got exactly what I needed.

My instincts were so primal they were scary.

I let my head fall to one side to give him access to explore. "This doesn't happen to me. Ever."

He grasped my ass and pulled it flush with his body. "This happens to me all the time. Every damn time I see you," he grunted.

I nearly melted as I felt his hard erection press against my lower belly.

"I never knew," I answered in a rush.

"Now you do," he answered abruptly. "The question is... are you game for a new adventure, a different dimension of our relationship?"

I knew he was asking me if I was okay with our friendship moving to a whole different level. "I'm scared," I confessed. "I'm not used to feeling this out of control."

"You'll have to get used to it, and trust me," he said as he slowly backed away and started to tug me into the deeper water.

I leaped onto his back and pushed his head underwater play-fully. "I've always trusted you," I told him as he surfaced.

I squealed as he lifted my body and tossed me so far that I was sputtering when I came up.

But he was there to lift me up and adjust my legs around his hips as he replied. "I want to make you come until you can't remember your own name anymore."

I ground my sex against his washboard stomach as I melted, knowing that I wanted exactly the same thing.

For this stolen period of time when we were alone in another part of the world, Zeke was my everything.

Let it happen. I heard his voice in my head, even though he hadn't spoken, and I laid my head on his shoulder.

The way I felt at the moment, I was helpless to do anything else but let him in.

CHAPTER 8

Lia

Two days later, I found myself wondering how I'd never known that Zeke was a pretty romantic guy.

Not in a sappy way, but in an I-want-you-to-remember-this-experience kind of way that touched my heart.

"I love it," I murmured to him as I clutched at the pendant he'd just put around my neck, a medallion that was carved in white gold, and inspired by the Mayan calendar to remind me of the ruins we'd explored all day.

We'd come back to our suite and ordered room service, which hadn't arrived yet. Zeke had wanted to give me my birthday present, even though it wouldn't technically be my birthday until midnight.

The gorgeous pendant had been a surprise that had nearly left me speechless.

The last few days had been magical, everything a couple could want on a honeymoon. Well, minus the sex part.

Zeke was attentive and affectionate, but he hadn't pushed for anything more than I wanted to give.

Truth was, I wanted to give him everything, and I knew that was dangerous.

This relationship is not permanent, which scares the hell out of me.

Every moment I spent with him was both heaven and hell. He made me happy, but I was terrified what would happen when it was over.

For me, every touch, every brush of our bodies, was too much to handle without wanting to beg him to fuck me, but his long-ago rejection still played in my mind.

I didn't feel like things were make-believe anymore. We both wanted more, and I was convinced that Zeke wanted to explore something more intimate. And I really wanted to know what it would be like to be with him.

I wanted the experience without the danger, but those two things went hand-in-hand.

The sexual chemistry and the resulting tension had me on edge.

"Thank you for today," I said as I turned around to face him.

"You mean you really enjoyed slugging around a bunch of ancient ruins?" he asked with a grin.

I smiled. "I did. I can't explain it, but I could almost feel the souls of Maya there. Is that weird?"

He shook his head. "It's a little eerie. But fascinating, too. They built great civilizations only to see them fall, and the culture die out. It's pretty amazing to see relics of a society that existed so long ago."

I nodded, knowing that Zeke understood my weird fascination. In fact, we'd always seemed to see history in the same way.

"So what's on the schedule for tomorrow?" I was starting to look forward to experiencing something different every day.

"Whatever you want. This is your time. And tomorrow is your birthday."

I put a hand on my hip. "I want you to enjoy it, too."

"I have a confession to make," he answered in a sincere, mesmerizing baritone. "There isn't much I'm not going to like if we're together."

I melted from the heat in his eyes. "I'm willing to do just about anything."

"There's a catamaran trip I wanted to arrange so we could do some snorkeling."

"I'd love that," I replied excitedly. Honestly, I was good doing anything with Zeke, too, but getting into some great snorkeling waters was pretty appealing.

He nodded. "I'll hook us up. And then we can go explore the town. I have an idea where we might be able to get some good Mexican food."

We both loved Mexican cuisine, and we wanted something more authentic. "Sold!" I said with a laugh.

I watched his handsome expression change as he looked at me intently. "Do you know how good it sounds to hear you laugh?"

"Have I really been that bad?" I asked.

I'd been miserable with Stuart. Maybe I hadn't realized just how much while I'd been stressing about the wedding. But over the last few days, it had hit me that I really had changed.

Being with Zeke made me happy, which was so opposite from how I'd felt when I was with Stuart.

Zeke and I loved just being together.

And I guess I'd forgotten how it felt to be with somebody who accepted me without criticism.

"You look happier," Zeke replied.

Because I'm with you.

I sighed. "We were always like this when we were younger. I guess I just forgot what relaxation and fun was like."

"That won't happen again. I'll be here to remind you."

I sighed.

No more Stuart.

No more constant belittling or sarcasm.

No more demanding mother of my fiancé who never thought I was good enough for her son.

No more...fear.

I was finally starting to see how really bad things were in hindsight. I just wish I had wised up sooner.

"I nearly married him," I said in a horrified voice. "What was I thinking, Zeke? Was I so damn desperate for love that I was willing to turn myself inside out to make things work with him? Was I willing to give up myself to please him?"

He stepped forward and put his arms around me. "He was a master manipulator, Lia. For fuck's sake, don't blame yourself. You'll get over him."

I put my hands on his shoulders, and tipped my head up to meet his gaze. "I'm not in love with him anymore. I'm not sure I ever was. I don't need to get over *him*. I need to get over the fact that he played me so damn well. I have to figure out what in the hell is wrong with *me*."

"There's nothing wrong with you," Zeke rasped. "You're a loving, giving person. You always have been. You just met up with somebody who was willing to take complete advantage of those traits. It's not some kind of character flaw you have. It's his. The bastard."

I wanted to believe what Zeke was telling me, but deep inside, I knew so much of what had happened with Stuart was my fault. "But I should have been strong enough to stand up for myself. I thought I did, but I realize I let him separate me from my friends, even you. We've barely seen each other for the last few years if it didn't involve the coffee shop."

I hadn't even known what was really happening in Zeke's life. I'd completely missed the fact that he had broken things off with Angelique, and my relationship with him had been almost superficial. That hurt considering all we'd been through together over the years.

"I think I can take some of the blame for that, too," Zeke said, his gorgeous eyes reflecting more than a little remorse. "I didn't want to see you with Stuart, so I pretty much avoided us meeting up that way. It was easier to just see you at the shop."

I frowned. "Why?"

"Because he had something I wanted," Zeke said in a husky voice.

"What?"

"He had you, Lia."

My heart skittered as I looked at the tense expression on his face. Zeke was as serious as I had ever seen him. "I'm sorry. I should have been a better friend," I said in a rush.

"I should have told you that I envied what you were giving to a guy who didn't deserve you," he countered.

I diverted my gaze and stepped away from him to give myself some space.

Being too close to Zeke made me feel vulnerable, even though I knew he was the only person who really understood me.

Taking a seat on the couch, I tried to force my body to relax as I answered, "None of this was in any way your fault. I wanted to pretend that everything was okay with Stuart, when it never really was. I convinced myself that he was the one. But he never was. You know my insecurities better than anyone, and you've never tried to play on them. I guess it was unfathomable to me that somebody else would use them to manipulate me. I was an idiot."

Zeke sat down on the other end of the couch. "Nobody you care about should ever do that to you."

"Stuart did," I answered. "And he made me feel so small and imperfect that he turned it around until I thought that I was lucky to have him. I believed that everything that went wrong was my fault. God, I even hated myself because I couldn't satisfy him sexually."

Zeke lifted a brow. "Are you serious?"

I nodded. "Something is wrong with me, Zeke. I've always been way too cold to enjoy anything intimate."

"For God's sake, Lia. You've never been the least bit cold. Has it ever occurred to you that your previous partners just sucked?"

"There really haven't been all that many," I confessed. "But no, I haven't considered that. How can more than one guy be incompetent?"

"Pretty damn easily if they don't care about whether or not you're there with them when it's time to come," he grumbled.

"I don't orgasm," I admitted.

"Never?" he asked in a graveled voice.

"Not once when I was with someone."

"But you can get yourself off?"

"Yes."

I watched as Zeke closed his eyes and let his head fall back until it hit the wall behind the sofa with a loud *thunk.*

I wasn't certain, but the sound he released right before his head smacked the wall sounded suspiciously like a tortured groan.

CHAPTER 9
Zeke

I *should have never fucking asked her if she could get herself off.*

Our room service had come and gone, but I was still haunted by images of Lia naked, stroking herself to climax.

Fuck!

I hadn't touched Lia since that first day we'd sprinted for the sea from the beach. God knew I wanted to, but the more I recognized how damn vulnerable Stuart had left her, the less I wanted to rush anything.

My body wanted me to, but my brain was trying to get my dick in check.

I wish I had paid more attention to *exactly* what Stuart was doing to Lia. The bastard had taken every good thing about her, and twisted it into something bad.

It pissed me off that he'd been able to read her well enough to be able to make her feel like she was nothing.

Lia, she was *something*. And I knew I had to give her time to realize that all of the problems had been Stuart's.

Yeah. She was right. I *did* know her vulnerabilities, but I'd rather support her than tear her apart. Hell, I had a few of my own issues—namely my inability to stop wanting the woman I'd married. Or at least give myself enough time to re-build her trust.

I slammed my hand against the shower control, turning it off way harder than I needed due to my frustration.

I knew that I was no longer going to be able to settle for just having Lia's body.

Not happening—since I also wanted her heart.

I grabbed a towel and started to dry my body as I thought about some of the things she'd told me.

If it wasn't so damn tragic, I would have laughed out loud about her assumption that she was cold. She had an enormous heart. She just hadn't found the right man to give it to, somebody who would cherish the gift.

Lia hadn't changed like she thought she had.

She'd just had her confidence severely shaken by somebody who should have never been allowed to get close to her.

Maybe she *had* realized that she didn't love him.

However, the relationship had gone on too long not to do some damage.

I can wait to try to seduce her. She's my wife. I just need her to understand that to me, she's perfect. Always has been.

One of Lia's vulnerabilities revolved around the loss of her parents and her subsequent move to Washington after that. She'd adored her Grandma Esther, but I knew it had been difficult to lose her mom and dad, and then be taken away from everything that was familiar to her before she even got into high school.

Since she was strong, Lia had adjusted, but it had left some lingering insecurities about caring about people because she was afraid that they'd leave her, too.

Watching her try to come to terms with her grandmother's death had torn me up because I knew damn well that she was reliving those fears of being left alone. She'd had no family left, so her pain had been pretty severe.

Stuart had come into her life right after Esther had died, and I had to wonder whether she'd been trying to fill some empty place inside her.

Understandable, but not necessarily wise. I should have been there for her more, even if it was just to get her out of Stuart's clutches.

But I'd been too damn busy feeling sorry for myself because she'd chosen *him* instead of *me*. And I'd been licking my wounds because of it.

What I'd confessed to her earlier in the evening was true. I *had* been envious of Stuart, and I'd had no fucking idea how to handle it except for keeping my distance.

Yeah, I'd thought he was a dick, but I'd never been quite sure whether it was really an unbiased opinion since I'd coveted her myself.

I wrapped the towel around my waist, opened the door of the bathroom to let the steam out, and started to shave.

Logically, I knew it was going to take time for Lia to figure things out. She'd eventually realize that none of what happened was her fault. But I was going to have a hell of a hard time not just getting her naked and proving that she was *anything but* cold.

Plus, it was going to take me some time to not want to beat the shit out of Stuart for making Lia doubt herself.

He'd taken a woman who was still grieving, a woman who was still hurting from losing the only family she had left in the world, and had turned her inside out.

It took a real asshole to do something like that.

I'm going to have to be patient.

Problem was, I had all I could do not to touch Lia now that she was my wife.

My protective instincts toward her had always been strong, but now that she was mine, I was downright possessive.

I grimaced as I rinsed the razor and put it on the counter. *I think I need a drink. Or two.*

Lia had gone to bed early since we had an early snorkeling excursion scheduled.

But I knew I was never going to sleep. I was too wound up.

I walked through the bedroom and went to the small kitchen to pull out a beer. I chugged it down, tossed the bottle and then grabbed a second one and screwed the top off.

"Zeke?" I heard Lia's sleepy voice say my name softly.

I turned toward her voice, and saw her standing at the entrance to the kitchen.

"I couldn't sleep, either," she said as she walked toward the fridge barefoot.

My eyes followed her.

I recognize the red and white cotton shorts and the matching tank top she was wearing. I'd packed them. It was the only pair of pajamas I'd found.

"You okay?" I asked in a rough voice.

She pulled out a beer and tried to unscrew the top. When I saw her struggling, I snatched the bottle, removed it for her, and handed it back.

Lia looked adorably sleepy, her beautiful blonde hair tussled, like she'd been tossing and turning in bed.

She hopped onto one of the kitchen counters, and then her eyes ran over my towel-clad body boldly, an action that made my dick go on high alert.

I wanted her to want me, but when I caught the signals that she wanted me, too, it became damn near unbearable to stop myself from lifting her off the counter and taking her to bed.

"I think I am okay," she answered, and then swallowed a portion of her beer before she continued. "I messed up big time, didn't I?"

It wasn't the first time I'd heard her ask that question through the years, but her wistful tone and the sadness in her eyes nearly sent me over the edge. "Not your fault," I snapped out. "And you got the hell out of the situation before you married him."

"I think I was searching for something, and I wanted it so badly that I ignored all of the red flags."

I put my bottle down on the counter and moved forward, situating my body between her silken thighs. I took the bottle from her hands and put it down on the counter beside mine. "I'm so fucking sorry I wasn't there for you, Lia."

She wrapped her arms around me and squeezed. "I wasn't there for you, either," she said with a sigh. "We drifted apart. And now I don't know what to do."

Love me!

I couldn't make that suggestion right now, but I sure as hell wanted to say it.

If she gave me her heart, I'd never fuck it up. Not anymore. I'd been too damn close to losing her.

"What do you want to do?" I was distracted by the feel of her soft body leaning into mine, but I'd gotten the question out.

"I just want to be with you," she said hesitantly. "I don't quite understand exactly what's happening, but I want you, Zeke. I'm just…scared."

Every protective, possessive, out-of-control instinct I had for her started to come to the surface. "It's me. We've known each other for a long time. Don't you know that you never have to fucking be afraid of me?"

"I'm not afraid of *you.* I'm afraid of the way I feel, and the last thing I want is for you to be disappointed."

"You never disappoint me, Lia. Never," I said in an animalistic tone I didn't recognize.

"First time for everything," she said, sounding uncomfortable.

I tightened my arms around her waist. I knew I wasn't willing to wait another night. Lia needed to learn just how warm she could be, and there wasn't another guy who could teach her about that but me.

I'd make her feel wanted.

I'd make her feel special.

And I'd damn sure make sure she was satisfied before my dick ever saw the light of day.

"Say the word," I demanded, clenching my fists while I sweated it out.

She was silent for a moment before she said quietly, "Word."

All of the tension drained out of my body. It wasn't the first time she'd said that, and I knew it was a sign that she was willing.

I didn't hesitate to put my hands under her ass, lift her up so she had to wrap those beautiful legs around me, and carry her to my bedroom.

CHAPTER 10

Lia

Every single negative thought flew out of my brain as I pressed my body against Zeke's. It was replaced with heat, desire, and anticipation, more pleasant feelings that I'd much rather focus on at the moment.

I'd laid in bed for over an hour, wondering what would happen if I just didn't think about the repercussions of screwing my best friend. Unfortunately, not a single scenario could block out the fact that I desperately wanted Zeke to fuck me until we were both sated.

Maybe he was right. Maybe I wasn't really cold. Maybe I just needed...him.

I'd gotten up to try to find something that would put me to sleep.

And then I'd seen Zeke in only a towel, and my mind had strayed to thoughts of releasing it until I could see all of him, touch every inch of him. Once the wicked thoughts had entered my head, I couldn't get rid of them.

Zeke was the most perfect specimen of manhood I'd ever laid eyes on, and he was mine. Even if it was only temporary, I couldn't ignore the sensual temptation of exploring my sexuality with him.

Just let it happen.

I relaxed as he let my feet touch the floor in the bedroom, but I kept my arms around him like I was afraid he'd disappear into thin air.

"I feel like I've waited forever for this," he said, his voice hoarse and unsteady.

My heart was kicking against my chest wall as I looked up and met his unflinching stare. "Me, too," I confessed.

He stepped back and reached for my tank top, and then pulled it over my head. I was bare beneath it, but I didn't hesitate to lift my arms so he could proceed with getting me naked.

I was nervous, but for some reason, everything felt so normal, so natural with Zeke. And I needed him to touch me so desperately that I wasn't afraid.

"You're so damn beautiful, Lia," he said in a deep voice that rolled down my spine, sending electric impulses to every single nerve.

My breath hitched, and I reached for his towel. "I want to see you," I answered. "I want to touch you, Zeke."

"Not yet," he said sharply, nudging my hand away as soon as the towel fell to the floor. "If you do that, I won't be able to focus on what's really important."

I tried to step back so I could see him, but he picked me up way too fast and carried me to the bed.

"What else could be more important?" I asked breathlessly as my back hit the sheets.

Zeke came down on top of me, but he didn't let me take his weight. He put more of it on his powerful arms as he hovered over me. "I want to see you come, Lia. It's just about the only thing I want right now."

His words made me shudder, and I moaned as his mouth covered mine.

Every bit of suppressed desire leaped from my body and took over my actions.

I no longer cared about the outcome. All I wanted was Zeke.

His kiss was ravenous, hungry in a way I'd never experienced before.

He demanded, and I happily gave, losing myself as I tangled my fingers in his gloriously coarse hair.

I got drunk on his masculine, musky scent, breathing him in as I tried to absorb his essence into every pore of my skin.

I was finally touching him, and I'd never felt anything so seductive.

"Zeke," I whimpered as he finally released my lips so I could speak.

"Don't think about anything, Lia. Just feel," he commanded, his mouth leaving trails of flame as it moved down my neck.

I loved the feel of our heated skin pressed together, and I was drunk on the pleasure of my hard nipples abrading against his chest.

When he pulled away, I nearly begged him to come back.

Until I felt his hands cupping my breasts, his thumbs circling the hard peaks of my nipples.

"Yes," I hissed. "Touch me. Please."

I can't say that he was gentle, his firm touch coaxing every sinful sensation he could get from me. But the last thing I wanted was a tepid fuck.

If anything, I wanted more.

My back arched as he took a hard peak in his mouth, his teeth scraping against the sensitive flesh as his other hand continued to manipulate the other nipple.

When he nipped, I squeaked, and then let out a tremulous sigh as his tongue stroked over the tip he'd just bit.

The pleasure/pain of the action fueled my need, and I felt moist heat pooling between my thighs.

Pressure started to build in my lower abdomen, and it started to knot tightly from the pleasure of Zeke's relentless assault.

"I need…more," I said, not caring if I sounded greedy.

"I'm going to give you everything you need, sweetheart," he growled as his mouth traveled into the valley between my breasts, and then down to my abdomen.

He pulled the shorts from my hips, and eased them down as he knelt between my legs.

Every inch of my skin felt like it was on fire, and my muscles were tense as I waited for him to come over me and fuck me.

But what I'd expected didn't happen.

Instead, he spread my legs wide, and I shivered as the cool air wafted across my vulnerable pussy.

I moaned as I felt his fingers brush against the pink flesh.

"You're so damn wet, Lia. So damn responsive. So hot. I can't wait to taste you."

I startled. I suddenly realized why he was settling between my legs instead of fucking me. "You don't have to do that," I said nervously.

No man had ever put their mouth on me. And I was trembling with anticipation. But Stuart had hated oral sex…unless I was sucking on him. He'd never been willing to do the same to me.

"I want to. I have to," Zeke said insistently. "Let me, Lia. I guarantee you'll like it."

All thoughts of protest flew out of my brain as his tongue stroked over the quivering pink flesh. He owned it in one long, satisfying swipe.

"Oh, shit, Zeke. Oh, my God!" The words left my mouth on a moan, and my hands speared into his hair as I held onto him for dear life.

He groaned against my flesh, and the vibration almost made me jump out of my skin.

I flopped back against the pillow and closed my eyes, letting my body just enjoy every sensual sensation.

I'd never experienced this level of intimacy, this much pure carnal emotion. And I savored it because it was so damn good.

"Yes," I moaned. "Please."

I felt the knot in my belly begin to loosen.

Zeke put his hands under my ass and lifted me so he could explore every single inch of my pussy.

It was both torture and bliss every time he brushed against the small bundle of nerves that needed more attention.

"Zeke," I pleaded as I yanked on his hair.

I yelped when his teeth bit down gently on my clit, gasping as I finally got what I needed, his teeth and tongue playing my body like a violin.

My climax rolled over me like a freight train. There was no slow build. My orgasm pummeled me as Zeke continued to lap at the juices that spilled from me as I flew over the edge.

"Oh, my God. Yes!" I screamed as I fisted his hair to keep my body from flying into space.

When it was over, I was left panting and helpless on the bed as Zeke slowly moved up my body.

I felt every movement, the connection of our bodies as he moved over me.

"You taste sweeter than I could have imagined," he rasped as his face moved into my vision.

I searched his eyes, but I couldn't see one inkling of revulsion. In fact, he looked like he'd enjoyed every second of his time between my thighs. And he still looked incredibly hungry.

I wrapped my arms around his neck as he swooped down to kiss me.

I tasted Zeke.

I tasted myself.

I tasted sinful, wicked pleasure.

And dammit! It was the sweetest, most delicious thing I'd ever tasted before in my life.

"Fuck me," I insisted as he ended the embrace.

"So demanding," he said with a hint of humor, though his eyes were so intent that it pinned me to the pillow.

I wrapped my legs around his waist. "Are you complaining?" I said as I lifted my hips to grind against him, my body ravenous to feel him inside me.

He reached down and positioned himself as he groaned, "Hell, no. I just want you to feel just as damn desperate as I do."

"Mission accomplished," I said with a strangled sound of need.

"Thank fuck!" he answered.

With one swift, powerful movement, he buried himself to his balls inside me.

I gasped as he stretched me. It didn't hurt, but I was hard-pressed to take his length and girth.

"You're so big," I said breathlessly.

"Are you okay?" His voice was suddenly concerned.

"If you stop, I'll never forgive you," I warned.

He gently pushed the hair from my face. "This has to be good for you, too, Lia. If it isn't, there's no reason to keep going for me."

Tears welled up in my eyes as I met his gaze. His blue eyes were liquid and molten. But I could see that he really meant what he said, and it touched a place so deep in my heart that it took me by surprise. "You mean that," I whispered.

"Of course I do. I need you with me."

I reached up and stroked his clean-shaven jawline. "You're so amazing, Zeke."

He was trying to say that my pleasure was his, and I knew his pleasure was mine. We were so damn connected that it made my heart ache.

"Right now I'm impatient," he answered gutturally. "Talk to me, sweetheart. Communicate with me. I have to know that you want this as much as I do."

The stretching sensation was no longer uncomfortable, and the need for him to fuck me was almost unbearable.

"I need you," I said simply, grinding up against him again.

"You have me," he ground out as he pulled back until he was almost out, and then thrust his enormous cock back inside me again with a little more force.

"Then show me," I begged. "Because there's nothing I need more than for you to fuck me like you mean it."

"I mean it," he grunted, and then began to move in a rhythm that left me mindless.

I moaned, my hands trying to touch every bare inch of his skin as he claimed my body in a way I'd never thought possible.

I felt him.

I tasted him.

I wallowed in Zeke.

Every thrust a relief and a torment and my body responded to him with sublime gratification.

I reveled in every stroke of his cock, my hips lifting to receive him every single time.

My legs tightened around him, and I ground against him every time he buried himself deep.

"Harder," I cried. "Please."

The feel of Zeke was addictive, and my body greedily wanted everything he had to give me.

He obliged me by moving hard. Faster. His movements so quick and rapid that I couldn't keep up. So I just hung on.

"Come for me, Lia. Let go," he persuaded and commanded.

I love you. God, I love you so much.

I wanted to say the words aloud, but I couldn't get them out because I was in the throes of another orgasm, a climax that was ripping at my soul as much as it was tearing through my body.

"Zeke!" I cried out, unable to get another word past my lips.

My core clenched hard, and spasmed powerfully around his cock.

"Fuck. Lia," he groaned as I milked him to his own release.

He kissed me, and I was speechless by the time we ended the frantic embrace.

I was a panting, shaking mess when he rolled me on top of him and held me, our bodies slick with sweat.

It wasn't like I didn't want to say something, but I was so stunned that I didn't know what to say.

Zeke had just proved to me that I wasn't the least bit cold.

I'd just always been with the wrong guys.

"Okay?" he asked in a deep, throaty voice.

"Definitely okay," I answered as I buried my face in his warm neck.

He stroked a hand over my back in a slow, soothing motion that was almost decadent.

I moved to his side and cuddled against him, reveling in the feel of his hot, powerful body against mine.

For the first time in a long time, I felt safe. And I felt wanted.

As I drifted off to sleep, I felt like I was finally exactly where I belonged.

CHAPTER 11
Lia

*I*t took me until our last day of our trip to realize that I'd *always* been in love with my best friend.

After Zeke's humbling rejection of me on my twenty-first birthday, I'd just never wanted those emotions to see the light of day ever again.

Any guy I would have ended up with would have been the wrong one, even if he'd treated me better than Stuart had.

If I wanted to be honest, I'd known for a very long time that I'd never really love anyone but Zeke, but since he hadn't wanted me, I'd been determined to bury those emotions so deep that they'd never rear their ugly heads again.

Zeke had proved to me, over and over again, that there was nothing wrong with me. In fact, he seemed to enjoy demonstrating it on every surface of our gorgeous suite.

Every time he touched me, I became bonded just a little deeper to him, and even though I was scared, I didn't regret letting it happen. If I was only going to get one shot at being with him for a little while, I was going to take it.

"You look deep in thought, beautiful," Zeke said as he came out onto the balcony where I was having my morning coffee.

I shook my head. "I was just enjoying the view. It's so beautiful here."

We had a glorious room that faced the ocean, and it was calming to wake up to the turquoise-colored Caribbean every day.

My eyes ran lovingly over his commanding form, wondering if I'd ever get used to the fact that this beautiful man was temporarily mine. His hair was mussed up because he'd just climbed out of bed, but he'd never looked more gorgeous.

I watched as he poured himself a coffee and sat down at the table with me.

"How do you manage to look incredibly hot when you just rolled out of bed?" I asked him with a smile.

He shrugged his strong shoulders as he replied, "Probably the same way you manage to look so beautiful right now."

He said the words so sincerely that they flustered me. I reached up and ran a hand through my messy hair. "I have bedhead. You don't," I argued.

"I'm too damn distracted to notice," he grumbled. "All I can think about is how you look when you come."

I laughed. For some reason, Zeke could always throw me off-balance with his blunt comments.

"Mind out of the gutter, Mr. Conner," I teased.

"I guess I'm still disappointed that I woke up without you in my bed," he answered.

"Don't you ever want a reprieve?" I joked.

"Hell, no," he said with a grin.

God, I loved his wicked smile. It made me want to take my clothes off and drag him back to bed.

But I knew we had plans for the day. We had a full day planned, consisting of swimming in underground caves, and zip-lining.

"I'm going to miss all this," I said wistfully. "It's been so perfect."

Being in Playa had been like a fairy tale. It mostly had to do with the man I was visiting here with, but the setting had been...magical.

Maybe I was afraid that everything would change once we were back in Seattle. It wasn't like we were going to separate right away, but it was bound to happen once we'd gotten our fill of mind-blowing sex.

I always knew this was temporary.

I just wished that knowing all this was happening for a limited time didn't hurt so much.

"Nothing is going to change," Zeke said. "We can still have sex in Seattle. But I'll miss it here, too. Things will be crazy once we get back."

I nodded. "I'd still like to open a second store once I pay you back."

"You don't need to pay me back, Lia. We're married. What's mine is yours."

Until we aren't together anymore.

"I want to," I argued. "Please." It was important to me to be able to hand him a check. I'd been giving him installment payments off my profits, but he'd trusted me when he'd turned over that much money to help me achieve my dream. And I wanted to make good on the loan.

"If that's what you feel like you need to do to be happy, I'm not going to stop you," he said, sounding slightly disappointed.

"It is," I confirmed. "If there's one person in the world I don't want to let down, it's you."

"You never have, and you never will," he said huskily. "Come here."

His eyes were beckoning, and I couldn't ignore the temptation. I rose, moved to his chair, and he promptly sat me down onto his lap.

I put my arms around his solid, massive shoulders to support myself, and his strong arms wrapped tightly around my waist.

"Thank you for this trip," I said softly. "It gave me a chance to get my head on straight."

"Damn! I thought you were thanking me for all those orgasms."

I laughed. "Do you ever think about anything except sex?"

"When you're around…no," he answered bluntly.

I savored the feel of his body against mine. Just being with him felt so…right.

Maybe it should have felt weird because we'd been friends for so long. Instead, things actually flowed like a natural progression of our relationship.

I'd known Zeke for so long that there was very little I didn't know about him. And vice versa. Adding the sexual element had just made it seem new.

I tilted my head down to look at him, and my heart skipped a beat as our gazes met and locked.

There was something incredibly personal about the moment, a message in his stare that I couldn't quite understand.

"Are you okay?" I questioned in a shaky voice, unable to stop trying to figure out the silent communication.

His eyes seemed to suddenly shutter, and the moment was gone. "I'm good."

"I guess I should go jump in the shower and get ready to go," I said, unable to keep the longing I felt out of my tone.

He let me go as I stood. "Need somebody to wash your back?" he asked hopefully.

"Pervert," I accused.

"Tease," he shot back in a teasing tone.

I folded my arms in front of me. "All I said was that I was going to get ready."

"Which means you're planning on taking off those pajamas. Any time you're getting naked, I want to be there," he replied.

"You're hopeless," I said in an amused voice.

"I like to think I'm hopeful."

I snorted, unable to resist him when he was in a playful mood. The need to be close to him was so strong that I said, "We won't get out of here early."

"I can be quick."

I rolled my eyes. If there was one thing Zeke Conner couldn't do, it was hurry an orgasm. The man tormented me until I couldn't take it anymore before he finally pushed me over the edge.

He said he never rushed a good thing.

And I had to agree with him. He never did quickies.

"Now that's something I might have to see to believe."

It was hopeless. I couldn't get enough of him, even if we had spent half the night burning up the sheets.

I slid through the door of the balcony.

Zeke rose and followed me so fast that he grasped my hand on his way, and ended up pulling me toward the master bedroom bath.

Turned out that I was right.

He didn't rush anything.

But it was certainly worth being late to our planned destinations for the day.

CHAPTER 12

Lia

Zeke had been right about nothing changing much when we arrived back in Seattle.

Really, nothing was different except for the scenery. We didn't spend as much time together because we were both back to work, but once we got home, the craziness between us just continued on. Zeke and I had been back home for a week, and we craved each other like we were still in Playa.

"You're quiet," Ruby observed as she arranged some of her amazing pastries in the glass case. "Is everything okay?"

My shop was small enough that I closed down for an hour during midday for lunch and restocking. Normally, I'd restock Ruby's pastries myself, but she'd stopped in to bring some heavenly Korean food for lunch.

We'd wolfed it down before I started getting things ready for the next rush of coffee lovers.

My manager was working out well, but she had the day off. So I was running the shop solo today.

"Stuart is coming by to pick up his ring. He apparently wants to give it to the new woman in his life."

Ruby slammed the full case closed. "Asshole," she snapped. "An engagement ring is special. They aren't made to be recycled."

I shrugged. "He doesn't feel the same way. And I have no problem returning it." The ring was gaudy and ostentatious, expensive, but it had never been my style.

My hand went reflexively to the ring currently on my finger, the gorgeous diamond that I'd recently learned was one of a kind. Because Zeke knew me, it was so perfect, and had quickly become a part of me. A symbol of the relationship I had with Zeke.

I kept replenishing cups and lids as Ruby said, "Are you going to be okay? It's the first time you've seen him in a long time."

I smiled at her. "I'm good. Stuart doesn't own me anymore."

"He never did," she answered adamantly.

"Maybe not," I agreed. "But looking back on it, I felt like a prisoner."

"God, I'm so glad you ended up with Zeke."

"Me too," I confided. "Even if it's only temporary."

Ruby put a hand on her hip and stared me down. "Why does it have to be? You love him, right?"

I nodded. "I do. But he's going to get tired of the hot sex eventually."

"Lia, there's a lot more to your marriage than sex. You've been friends forever. You know each other. You understand each other. If that isn't a great relationship, I have no idea what is. If you love him, it's perfect."

"I think I always have loved him. I was just in denial because the man I really wanted would never be available."

"I don't get it. Zeke adores you. And you're married to him now."

I startled as I heard someone pounding on the door.

I turned my head to see Stuart waiting impatiently at the locked door. "He's here," I said, unable to completely brush off the twinge of fear that zinged through my body as I looked at him.

"We can talk later," Ruby said. "Are you okay being alone with him? Do you want me to stay?"

"This is something I think I need to do alone," I replied.

Ruby nodded. "I'll be around. I'm here if you need me."

My heart swelled with love for the younger woman. Ruby had been a steadfast friend who never judged. She was just always... there for me.

I moved forward and hugged her tightly before I followed her to the door. "Thank you," I said in a quiet voice as I unlocked the door.

She shook her head. "Don't thank me. You've done a lot for me, Lia. You gave me purpose when I needed it, and you've encouraged me to keep doing what I loved. I'm happier, and I'm healing because of your friendship. You never have to thank me for being your friend."

Ruby had grown so much over the course of our friendship that she was almost unrecognizable as the timid woman who had offered to help me find better products for my store.

She'd blossomed tremendously because Jett had stood beside her, loved her unconditionally, and encouraged her every step of the way.

My eyes lifted to see Stuart right in front of me as I pulled the key from the lock.

My relationship with my ex had been a far cry from what I had now with Zeke, and what Ruby had with Jett.

I flinched as he pushed on the open door, nearly knocking me on my ass.

Ruby slipped out as Stuart barged in. I locked the door behind him since I had some time until I re-opened.

"I'll get the ring," I told him stoically as I headed toward the counter.

"You're looking elegant as usual," he said in a sarcastic tone. "My God, Lia. When are you going to learn to present yourself as a woman instead of a sloppy child?"

I reached behind the counter and snatched the box from the place that I'd left it, and then moved back to Stuart again.

It wasn't the first time I'd heard his criticism about the way I dressed for work. My place was a casual one and I was wearing a pair of jeans, a pretty jade sweater, and a pair of sneakers that didn't kill my feet by the end of a twelve-hour day.

One of his biggest complaints had always been the ponytail that I always sported to keep my hair out of my way while I was running around the store.

"Luckily, the way I look or act isn't really your concern anymore." I held out the boxed ring, anxious to get rid of it… and Stuart.

He snatched the offering, popped open the lid to make sure the ring was there, and then dropped it into his pocket. "You can't blame me for looking for something better," he said in the critical voice I hated. "Look at you. You have very little higher education, and you spend your entire day as nothing more than a barista."

My temper started to flare, and that was something that had never happened before when Stuart was berating me. I'd kept it buried to avoid an escalation of his humiliation.

I was afraid of him. I was always scared. I sensed that things could get physical if we argued.

The sudden realization of my true fears slammed into me with a force that rocked my body, and I tensed up more.

Stuart was an abuser. Maybe he'd never done anything except shove me around occasionally. But I was starting to understand how much the verbal abuse had scarred me, even though he'd never really hurt me physically.

"I'd rather be a barista than a common bully," I shot back at him.

"I thought maybe you preferred to be a slut since you married another man within a few days of our wedding," he said angrily. "Not that you really have any skills at satisfying a man. That's one of the reasons I wanted another woman."

Every single mean word he'd ever said to me rose up to the surface, as my hand flew through the air, landing with a satisfying *smack* as it connected with his face.

Fueled by fury, the slap had snapped his head to one side, and I felt nothing but gratification as I watched his face turn red with wrath.

"You think you found a better woman?" I asked angrily. "Well, I found a way better man, too. I'm glad I didn't marry you, and I feel sorry for the next bride you have lined up."

"You ungrateful bitch," he hissed. "I made you. You were nothing before I took pity on you."

"I wasn't nothing," I informed him as I strode to the door. "I was something. And you tried to beat me down until I thought I was the one with the problems. But it didn't work."

Maybe Stuart had bent me, but he had never broken me. It had just taken the affection of a better man to remind me that I had been okay just the way I had been. And his nasty comments about how cold I was couldn't even break the surface anymore. I knew better.

I shoved the key into the door. "Get out. We're done here," I said briskly.

"You fucking hit me!" His voice boomed around the small space.

"It's nothing compared to what you deserve. You're a bully, you're abusive, and you're a twisted prick. I want nothing except your absence."

I'd be damned if I'd show him even a twinge of fear. I was done with that.

"You'll be lucky if I don't sue you," he snarled.

I shrugged. "Feel free. I have the best defense attorney in the country as a husband."

I opened the door and waited for him to exit. I wasn't about to flinch, even though my heart was racing with fear that he might try to physically hurt me.

Stuart was not a guy who let anything he perceived as an insult go unpunished, but he'd definitely made me pay enough for the last few years.

My body was tense as I watched the indecision on his furious face.

I could tell he wanted to get his revenge, but because I wasn't willing to back down, he was hesitating.

"Get. Out," I said firmly.

"Someday, you'll get what you deserve," he rasped as he left the store.

"I already did," I said softly as I quickly locked the door behind him.

I had Zeke, and maybe he was more than I deserved, but I never felt inferior to him. He didn't hurt me. He didn't try to make me into something I was not.

Tears of relief started to trickle down my cheeks, with the realization that I made a pretty lucky escape.

I leaned against the door and swiped away the tears, determined that once I'd let go of my anger with a good cry, Stuart would never be allowed to take up space in my brain ever again.

CHAPTER 13

Lia

I felt so much lighter the next day as I pulled into the parking garage of Zeke's penthouse, surprised to see that his Range Rover was already in his parking spot.

I'd knocked off early since my manager was on duty, and I picked up some groceries so I could make Zeke chicken parmesan with pasta, his favorite.

Cooking for him was never a chore since he went out of his way to let me know how much he appreciated it.

Other than the fact that I was afraid that our relationship would eventually end, I was happy.

After my encounter with Stuart, I was moving on. He no longer had any power over me, and I was done being afraid. Maybe I'd have some lingering self-doubt for a while, but I knew it would fade away.

I shut off the engine of my car, and gathered up the grocery bags.

But I hesitated to leave my vehicle as I spotted a familiar figure making her way to her own vehicle.

Angelique.

Here. At Zeke's apartment building.

My heart squeezed in my chest as I connected her presence with the fact that she was parked in the garage of Zeke's building.

We'd only met a few times in passing, but she was a woman very few people would forget.

She was always immaculately groomed, and she reminded me of a woman who spent a lot of time on her appearance. Her long, dark hair was always perfect, and she had to be an ethnic mix because she had an exotic look that most men probably found irresistible.

I let go of a shaky breath as she left, but I couldn't let go of the jealousy that had come to life with a vengeance.

She was here.

She'd obviously been with Zeke.

Was he seeing her again?

I fought the doubts that were creeping in, but as I rode the elevator to the penthouse, I knew I wasn't totally successful at brushing them aside.

"Lia," Zeke said hoarsely as he wandered out of the bedroom with only a pair of pajama pants riding low on his hips.

I put the groceries on the counter before he could reach for them.

Zeke didn't usually hang out in pajama pants unless he'd just gotten out of bed, and the thought of anybody being in his bed except me made me feel defeated.

He was never really mine. I knew that.

But the fact that our relationship was only temporary did soften the blow that Zeke was apparently sleeping with Angelique again.

"I saw Angelique," I said in a resigned tone. "You could have just told me that you wanted out of this marriage before you found somebody else to screw."

I started putting the groceries away, but I wanted to just sink onto the floor and weep.

"I don't know what you're saying," he said in a harsh voice.

I turned to face him. "I'm saying that I saw Angelique leaving the building. Are you sleeping with her?"

"No." His answer was simple.

"Then why was she here?" A glimmer of hope sparked in my soul, but I was too defensive to let it turn into anything else.

I was surprised when he pushed me against the refrigerator, forcing it to close before he pinned me with his body.

"Are you seriously trying to say that you think I was screwing another woman?" he asked harshly.

I looked up at him. "I don't know what to think. She was here. And you're dressed...like that. I didn't even think you'd be home yet."

He slammed a fist against the stainless-steel fridge above my head. "Jesus, Lia! After the last few weeks, you still don't fucking believe that I fucking love you. There *is no* other goddamn woman for me. I know I wasn't the greatest of friend to you while you were with Stuart, but I've tried every fucking thing I know how to do to let you know how damn sorry I was. I know I let you down, but I don't know how in the hell to convince you that I'm not going anywhere, and I'll never touch another woman. I can't. I love you too damn much."

I lost track of how many curse words he'd managed to put into one declaration, but it didn't really matter. I was way too focused on three little words he'd never said before.

He'd been staring into my eyes as he'd told me that he loved me, and I felt the truth in what he said deep into my soul.

Zeke never lied to me. And I didn't think he was capable of it when he was looking into my eyes while he spoke.

"I don't understand," I stammered. "She was here, and you're here with hardly any clothes on."

"You're pretty hot when you're jealous," he commented softly.

I felt like a little green monster had temporarily taken up residence in my body as I said, "I wonder why Angelique was here."

"She works here occasionally at the front desk. I saw her when I came in. That's how we initially met."

I felt my muscles relax. I was still pinned against the refrigerator by Zeke's warm body, but I wasn't trying to get away.

"I'm sorry. I'm so sorry," I blurted out. I felt terrible for even thinking that Zeke would betray me. If he'd wanted all this over with, I knew he would have just told me. But I'd gone with a knee-jerk reaction because I loved him so much it hurt.

"It's okay," he said he moved back. "I get a little crazy sometimes when it comes to you."

I finally got a good look at Zeke when he moved away, and I was dismayed when I saw that he was as pale as a ghost. "Are you okay?" I asked as I stepped up to him and put a hand to his face.

He was burning up.

"You have a fever," I said, worried as I looked him over steadily.

He nodded. "I knew I was coming down with a cold yesterday, but I went to the doc today because I was having a hard time swallowing. He gave me a shot in the ass and sent me home with antibiotics. I have strep."

"Oh, no," I said, feeling anxious because I'd made a sick man stand here and justify why he wasn't cheating on me.

Zeke didn't get sick. In fact, I didn't think I'd ever seen him anything but healthy.

I put my arm around him as I demanded, "Back to bed."

"Don't get too close," he ordered. "I'm contagious."

I rolled my eyes. "Move," I insisted, and I stayed beside him until he finally flopped back into bed. "I can't believe you didn't tell me right away."

"I hadn't planned on even getting close to you," he admitted glumly. "I don't want you sick, too."

My heart skittered as I realized that Zeke's every thought seemed to revolve around me. I sat down on the bed and stroked his wayward hair back from his forehead. "Get used to me being very close until you're feeling better."

He looked like hell, and it scared me. I wasn't used to seeing him anything but healthy.

He scowled at me. "And if I don't want you close?"

"Then I'll call your mom," I warned. "It's me or her. And it will pretty much be both of us since I don't plan on going away."

I knew the last thing Zeke probably wanted was his mother when he was ill.

"That's just cruel," he muttered as he put his arm over his head. "Did you even hear me when I said that I love you?"

"I heard you," I answered. "And you have no idea how happy that makes me because I love you, too, Zeke. But right now, I just want to get you better."

"Say it again," he demanded grumpily.

"I love you," I said obligingly.

He tried to crack a small smile. "I'm better."

I shook my head, but a small grin formed on my lips. "You're not getting out of bed. I'm going to see if I can talk your assistant into bringing me some things I can use to make some soup, and if you're a good boy, you can have ice cream," I teased.

He groaned. "It sucks to have the woman I love not see me as her stud."

"I don't need a stud," I argued. "I just need to see you healthy."

"We could play some naughty nurse thing."

I laughed at the hopeful look on his face. Even when he was this sick, Zeke was still trying to be upbeat.

"Maybe I'll find a costume when you're recovered," I answered happily.

I started to rise so I could call Zeke's assistant, but he grabbed my hand. "Lia," he said, his voice sounding like his throat had been scraped with sandpaper. "I really do love you. I didn't mean to blurt it out like that, but you have to already know how I feel."

His expression was so earnest that I felt like a vise was tightening around my heart. God, he was beautiful, even when he was sick as a dog. I leaned forward and kissed him on his heated forehead. "I really do love you, too. Now get some rest while I get some other groceries. I was going to make chicken parmesan, but that's not going to work right now."

I had a million questions I wanted to ask him, but I was more concerned about his health.

"If you get sick, I'm going to be really pissed off," he muttered as his eyes closed.

I smiled as I got to my feet, straightened up the bed, and shot him one last worried look as I left the bedroom.

Zeke had always been there for me. Now it was my turn. And I planned to do everything I could to make sure he got back on his feet again.

CHAPTER 14

Lia

Zeke was miserable through the first couple of days of his illness, and he was a terrible patient.

I'd had to stomp my foot down pretty hard to keep him in bed after the initial severity of his infection started to subside.

"I can't just lie here anymore, Lia. It's driving me crazy," he said on the fifth day. "At least let me go get a shower. You've been waiting on me for days now."

He was recovering, but judging by his occasionally unsteady gait when he was moving to the bathroom, I could tell he was still weak.

I put my hands on my hips. There was probably no reason he couldn't get up. His fever was gone, and I knew he was getting restless and frustrated. "I'm going in with you," I insisted.

He grinned up at me. "Do you really think I'm going to object?"

"No funny stuff, stud," I said adamantly. "I just want to make sure you aren't going to fall down while you're in there."

"I feel fine, sweetheart," he answered as he threw the covers back. "I have since yesterday."

I shooed him into the bathroom, and when he started to brush his teeth, I dashed back to strip the bed and put on clean sheets.

I hurried back into the bathroom and turned on the water of the rain shower, and then stripped off my clothes as I anticipated the warm water on my skin.

Exhaustion was taking over my body since I'd had little sleep. Not because Zeke had been demanding, but due to the fact that I'd been worried about him anyway.

Zeke had quickly become my world, and seeing him down and out had shaken me up enough to realize that I was going to have to spill everything to him. I owed him that. I had to tell him that I was pretty sure I'd always loved him, and ask him why he hadn't taken me up on my offer to be more than friends years ago.

But not right now.

I stepped into the water that fell like a gentle rain, and sighed as I watched him finish shaving.

He was the hottest man I'd ever seen, even if he was recovering from an illness. Dressed only in another pair of pajama bottoms that clung to his hips like a lover, I'd never seen a more gorgeous sight than Zeke.

I reached for the shampoo and body wash, making quick work of getting clean as Zeke entered the large space with me.

I'd dashed into the shower a couple of times, but it had been so quick that I hadn't really relaxed.

"You look tired," Zeke said unhappily as he got his entire body wet.

"I'm fine," I assured him. "It feels good to be able to relax. I was worried about you."

Done cleaning myself up, I opened my eyes and reached for the soap that Zeke used.

"I know when I have it good. I'm not planning on dying anytime soon," he answered gruffly.

My heart sped up as I filled my hands with his soap.

Was that what I'd been afraid of all along? Was I manifesting the fear that Zeke would somehow be taken away from me? That terror was irrational, and I knew it. He was young and healthy. But my parents hadn't been very old, and they'd been gone so suddenly that it was scary.

My grandmother had been older, but not really old enough to have left me so suddenly. Unfortunately, cancer was a greedy beast. And it had swept my grandma away in a matter of months.

"I don't want to lose you," I told Zeke bluntly as I started to soap up his body. "I'm not sure I'd survive if I did."

"I know you've lost everybody you ever loved," he said in a patient baritone. "But you're not getting rid of me that easily, Lia. I can't stand to think about anything happening to you, either. But life is kind of a crapshoot. And I'm a gambling kind of guy. I'd rather be with you and deal with whatever happens than to be without you my entire life."

I looked up at him steadily as I said, "Me, too."

Love was always a risk, but Zeke was worth taking a chance. I'd rather love him for as long as we both had, with no regrets.

He closed his eyes and leaned back against the tiled shower wall with a groan. "You're going to kill me now if you don't stop."

I'd finished his back, and was running my hands freely over his muscular chest and gloriously toned abs.

One glance lower, and I knew why he was complaining.

His cock was rock hard, and doing a full salute.

I didn't hesitate to move my hand down to wrap it around the enormous, steely shaft. "I can take care of this," I told him in a sultry voice that I couldn't control. "Relax."

"Not happening if you're touching me, baby," he rasped loudly.

I stroked his massive cock, my anticipation building as I watched his face.

He looked hungry.

He looked frustrated.

And he looked like he was mine to pleasure.

Everything with him always happened so fast that I'd never gotten the chance to just touch him, taste him, and I relished the opportunity.

"I love you," I said as I dropped to my knees.

"Fuck! I love you, too, sweetheart," he said in a desperate tone.

His words rushed through my body like adrenaline, but there was also a gentle peace that was right there beside the excitement.

I rinsed the soap from the hard shaft before I took him into my mouth.

I started off lazily, my mouth and tongue savoring him before I finally started to apply some suction.

His body jerked as my movements got rougher and rougher, my hands grasping his tight ass to move at a steady pace.

A feral sound left his mouth as he tangled his hand in my hair and guided me. "Touch yourself, Lia. I'm not going to last long."

I looked up and caught the carnal expression on his face. It spoke of lust, longing, and so much crazy love that my sex spasmed violently.

His eyes were pleading, so I took a hand from his tight butt cheek, and slid it boldly between my thighs.

There was no hesitance from me. I wasn't shy about giving us both what we wanted.

My fingers slid through the wet heat, and I shuddered as I rubbed over my clit.

I was primed and ready, my body as tight as a bow as I found a rhythm that felt good, and stayed with it while I continued to swallow Zeke's cock.

I felt his hand tighten in my hair, and when I looked up again, he was watching me, his gorgeous blue eyes molten and burning with an incendiary heat that consumed me.

We connected without words, and Zeke didn't take his eyes away until his head fell back and an animalistic growl was wrenched from his mouth.

The sexy sound sent shockwaves through my body, and I sped up my fingers, rubbing harder at the bundle of nerves as I felt my impending climax.

I moaned around Zeke's cock, and the vibrations set him off.

"I'm done for, Lia," he groaned. "Move back."

Was he crazy? I worked too hard to coax him to orgasm. I wasn't going to give up the chance to taste it.

I swallowed hungrily as Zeke exploded, reveling in his essence as it flowed powerfully down my throat before I finally let go and found my own release.

"Zeke," I said with a moan as pleasure flooded my body and my soul.

I relished the hot water flowing over my body as I panted on the tile, one hand gently stroking Zeke's cock and the other still between my legs.

He pulled me to my feet and wrapped his powerful arms around me as he said huskily, "Do you know how damn crazy you make me feel?"

"As crazy as you make me?" I asked in a mumbling voice.

I still hadn't completely recovered, so I laid my head on his shoulder.

"Crazier," he rumbled as his hands stroked over my soaked body, as though he was afraid I'd suddenly disappear. "Let's get out of here."

I didn't protest as he turned off the water and we stepped out. He toweled us both off before we collapsed together on the bed.

He pulled the covers up, and I cuddled up to his side when he protectively wrapped his arm around me like a vise.

"Are you okay?" I asked.

"Never been better," he teased. "Sleep, Lia. I'm not going anywhere."

I let out a sigh of contentment as my eyes drifted closed, and I did exactly what he told me.

I slept a very long, dreamless sleep that left me feeling normal again by morning.

CHAPTER 15

Zeke

The next morning, I sat in my home office, feeling pretty much normal. Maybe I still didn't have the stamina I usually had—which isn't an easy thing for a guy to admit—but I knew I'd get it back after a day or two out of bed.

I'd been awake since dawn, and I'd finally left Lia fast asleep in our bed, hoping the dark circles under her eyes and the anxious look on her face would both disappear.

Shit! I really hated the fact that she was so damn afraid of losing somebody she loved, but then, I couldn't blame her, either. Pretty much every important person in her life had died before their time, and I'd probably be just as terrified as she was if all of my family was suddenly gone before I'd turned thirty.

The only thing I could do was be there—and hopefully not get sick in the near future. Eventually, her fear would lessen. I knew that. She just needed some peace, and some time off from people dying on her.

The phone rang, and I snatched it from the charger before it rang enough times to wake Lia up.

A quick glance at the clock left me wondering who in the hell would be calling at nine a.m. "Conner," I said, assuming it was somebody from work.

"I'd like to speak to Lia Conner please," the male voice asked in a businesslike tone.

"This is her husband. She's not available." Okay, I was just a little bit edgy over the fact that any male was calling for my wife.

"Marvin Becker from Becker and Associates. I'm calling regarding Esther Harper's estate."

I relaxed. It was the attorney for Esther's estate. "Zeke Conner. How can I help you? I guess you could say I'm Lia's attorney."

I heard a bark of laughter coming through the handset. "I know you by reputation, Mr. Conner," the gentleman said with humor in his tone. "But I'm pretty sure your wife doesn't need a defense attorney. My business is pretty benign. Can you let her know that the estate is settled, and that I'm sending a check by courier? A package should arrive shortly with the monies owed and I think she needs to read the codicil and a personal letter that I was instructed to give her after everything was finalized."

"Esther left a codicil?" I balked a little at the thought.

"It's all in the package," he answered cagily.

"Is this going to upset my wife?" I said with a protective growl. "Because the last thing she needs is any more emotional turmoil."

"I don't think it will," he said hesitantly. "In fact, it might help. That's about all I can say."

While I appreciated attorney-client privileged information, it still irritated the hell out of me that he wouldn't say anything more.

I hung up, and tried to figure out what Esther had changed.

"Good morning."

I looked toward the sleepy, female voice, grinning as I saw her smiling from the entrance to the office.

I stood up. "Coffee? I already made some."

She nodded and retreated toward the kitchen.

Because I was hopeless at doing anything else, I followed her.

Unfortunately, she was no longer nude, and had pulled on a pair of pajamas very similar to the ones she'd worn in Playa—a pair of stretchy shorts and a tank top.

"Sit," she demanded, pointing at the barstool at the kitchen counter. "I can get my own coffee."

"I'm feeling good, Lia. I'm going back to work on Monday." It was Friday, so that gave me a few more days to work from home and make sure that I was no longer going to infect anybody else at the firm.

She nodded. "I'm going back to the shop on Monday, too. But I plan on making sure you take it easy over the weekend."

Her eyes no longer looked haunted, but she had a tenacious look on her face that was almost scary.

I grinned as I watched her stand on her toes to grab a mug that I could have easily reached, and then fill it with coffee.

I knew her routine by heart, and I no longer cringed when she added a ton of creamer to her coffee, and several spoons of sugar.

"Do you want some M&M's with that?" I joked.

She appeared to contemplate the possibility before she answered, "Maybe later."

"I'm pretty well stocked," I informed her.

I bought the candy in bulk, and I had several boxes in the cupboard. It had become my habit over the years. I never ran out of them.

She leaned over the counter, her face so close to mine that I had to stop myself from putting my hand behind her head and yanking her closer so I could kiss her.

"Do you know how incredibly sweet that is? The fact that you stock up on my favorite candy?" she asked quietly.

"It's not exactly a big deal," I answered.

"It's a big deal to me," she argued. "Sometimes it's the little things that go unnoticed, but they really are important."

"Like you staying home from your store to take care of me?" I questioned.

"You'd do it for me," she pointed out.

And hell, of course I would.

I was saved from answering by the sound of the buzzer from the lobby.

It was the courier, and I told the receptionist to let them come up.

After signing for the delivery, I took the package into the kitchen.

"Who was it?" Lia asked curiously from her chair at the table. She was finishing her coffee, the mug nearly empty already.

I sat across from her. "Courier. It's from the estate attorney."

"Open it," she requested. "You know more about all that legal mumbo jumbo than I do."

I pulled out the paperwork, handed her the check, and then scanned the documents.

"This is for you." I gave her the sealed envelope that I already knew contained a personal letter from Esther.

I quickly read the simple codicil. "Holy shit," I cursed.

"What?" Lia said anxiously. "Is something wrong?"

"No. But I never knew that Esther was quite this crafty. Lia, she was always going to give you everything she had. She added a codicil that states as much. For some reason, she didn't want you to know until you had passed your twenty-eighth birthday."

She frowned. "Why? Why would she do that?"

I nodded toward the envelope. "Read the letter. It will probably explain."

I was tense as she opened the missive and pulled out a single sheet of paper. I watched her face as she read.

The kitchen was silent as her eyes scanned the page, and then a giant tear plopped on top of the paper she was holding. And then another.

Finally, she dropped the letter and looked at me. "She knew, Zeke. She knew that you and I would end up together. This whole will was a charade to force us to figure out that we loved each other."

I whistled as I got up and moved around the table. "Pretty dangerous game she was playing. What if we hadn't ended up together?"

"She said she knew that we would, but she was afraid we'd never want to rock the boat on our friendship," she said in a tearful voice.

I lifted her up, and then sat back down with Lia's warmth cradled against me.

"She might be right," I confessed. "I never wanted to lose you, but I should have told you a long time ago that my feelings had changed. But then Stuart came along, and you weren't available anymore. I stayed away as much as I could. But I had to know that you were going to be okay."

"I almost wasn't," she murmured against my neck.

"Your marriage was never going to happen," I said harshly.

"Why?"

"Because I finally realized what an ass I was, and I was coming to find you when I found you in the hallway after you'd talked to Stuart's brother. I was going to do every single thing I could to talk you into canceling the wedding."

CHAPTER 16

Lia

*I*t took me a moment to really understand what Zeke was saying. "So you were looking for me so we could talk?"

He nodded. "I couldn't let you marry him, Lia. Not if I could possibly stop it. And I wasn't averse to bodily carrying you out of the chapel if I had to. It wasn't all about me, even though I knew at the chapel that I was in love with you. I wanted to keep you from making a mistake that might hurt you for a very long time."

I leaned back so I could see him, swiping a tear from my cheek. "I wasn't going to marry him, Zeke. When I got up the morning of my wedding, I was sick to my stomach. And once I was in the church putting on my wedding dress, it suddenly dawned on me that I couldn't go through with the wedding because I didn't really love Stuart. I was going to talk to Stuart so we could end it when his brother found me."

"So you really wouldn't have gone through with it?" he asked in an incredulous baritone.

I shook my head. "But I guess I had backup just in case I changed my mind. It's good to know you had my back."

I stroked a hand over his whiskered jawline, my heart so full of love that I never wanted to stop touching the amazing man I'd married.

"Maybe I was a little late, but I finally realized that I was lying to myself if I thought I was going to sit through the ceremony while you married somebody else. And somebody like Stuart? Not happening."

"Exactly how long were you lying to yourself?" I asked curiously.

"Years," he replied.

"I offered myself to you once, but you didn't seem to be interested." That night didn't hurt anymore, but I wanted to know exactly when we stopped really listening to each other.

"Your twenty-first birthday," he said in a raspy voice. *"Jesus, Lia. Did you really think I was going to take advantage of the fact that you were hammered? I was your friend."

"I knew exactly what I was doing, Zeke."

"You never mentioned it when you were sober," he grumbled.

"I was embarrassed. But I knew what I wanted. I just thought that it wasn't going to happen."

"Even then, I wanted it to happen," he admitted. "But I wasn't about to fuck you when you were two sheets to the wind, sweetheart. I cared too much about you to do that."

"We've really been dancing around each other all these years," I said with a sigh.

"Pretty much," he told me. "Why do you think I wanted to be the one to take you out on your twenty-first birthday? I didn't trust any other guy to be around you when your guard was down. But when you didn't talk about what you'd said the night before, I thought you'd forgotten everything that had happened while you were drunk."

"I never forgot," I confessed. "I was embarrassed because I thought you didn't feel the same way. After a while, I guess I buried it because I already assumed you didn't want me, and I didn't want to lose our friendship, too."

I squeaked as he stood up and dropped my ass on the table.

"Assumptions have gotten us both into trouble," he said roughly.

I nodded as I gazed up at him. "I know."

"No more guessing for either of us. If we want to know something, we ask."

"I'll talk to you," I agreed.

"And I want you to trust me, Lia. I want you to know that there isn't another person in this world as important to me as you."

"I shouldn't have accused you of seeing Angelique," I said remorsefully.

"No, you shouldn't have. But I get feeling possessive. In fact, you make me pretty damn crazy."

I opened my mouth to answer, but the words were stifled as his mouth covered mine.

Wrapping my arms around his neck, I let myself get lost in Zeke.

I wanted to climb inside him, and never come back out again. He surrounded me in passion and love so completely that I couldn't get close enough.

"Zeke," I panted as he released my lips. "Fuck me."

He pushed me back so I was sprawled out on the kitchen table like a buffet.

"You know, this whole bossy thing you've got going on makes my dick so damn hard that I can't think," he rasped as he pulled off my shorts.

He pulled me up and I wrapped my legs around his waist. "I'd be more than happy to give you a boner any time you want," I whispered against his neck.

"Do you know why it turns me on?" he questioned.

My body was taut with need, but I asked, "Why?"

"Because I know you're happy. I know that Stuart didn't fucking break your spirit. I know that you're feeling confident again. And I know that you fucking love me."

He moved back and surged inside me with a force that made me suck in a breath as he lodged himself deep.

"Yes," I said breathlessly. "I do love you, Zeke. So much."

"I love you, too, baby, even if you do make me lose my damn mind."

I melted into him then, luxuriating in every frantic thrust of his cock.

Now wasn't the time for anything except the frenzy of joining us together. And I wanted it just as hard and hot as I could get it. "More," I pleaded, my legs tightening around his waist.

He gave me more. Zeke gave me everything, and I felt myself hurtling toward climax as he grasped my ass, his cock pummeling into me with satisfying urgency.

Zeke was mine, and I felt it with every single movement he made.

He claimed me as his.

And I took what I'd wanted for so damn long, my body finally imploding as I shuddered through my release.

"You were always meant to be mine," Zeke growled as he started to come. "Always. Fucking. Mine."

I clung to him, my breathing ragged as his words sunk into my soul.

Maybe I hadn't known it when I was a kid, but I knew now that Zeke had always been my destiny.

My Grandma Esther was right.

"We were always meant to be together," I said breathlessly as I rested my head on his shoulder, our bodies still connected as we tried to recover from the quick, intense experience we'd just shared. "My grandma was right."

Zeke stroked a hand over my hair. "Maybe it was easier to see from the outside. But we always made sense, sweetheart. We just took the hard way to find each other."

I moved back and kissed him, a long, slow, exploring embrace that left me raw and vulnerable.

I put my arms on his shoulders, our faces still close together as I whispered, "I should have known from the moment you put Bobby Turner on the ground for trying to feel my boobs."

"I never knew his name, but I hated that little bastard," he said sternly. "You were only fourteen."

"And you were my hero," I shared with a smile.

"I always want to be your hero, Lia," he said earnestly.

"You never stopped being one to me," I answered. "I love you, Zeke."

"I love you," he answered immediately.

I hugged him tightly as he picked me up from the table and headed for the master bedroom.

"I don't think I'll ever look at breakfast the same way again," I muttered.

Although Zeke and I had tried out almost every surface of the penthouse, we'd never christened the kitchen table.

I smiled as he started to laugh, a sound that boomed through the house so loudly that my heart started to gallop wildly.

It had been a long time since I'd heard Zeke laugh like he was the happiest guy in the world.

Maybe I'd *never* heard that.

"I'm going to make you so happy," I promised. "We'll eventually forget all the hard stuff."

"I'm already happy," he rumbled. "And I'll have one more hard thing for you to deal with in another minute or so."

He dropped me on the bed, and I looked up at him.

His eyes were so full of love that I felt like I could hardly breathe because I loved him just as much.

"Bring it on, stud," I dared.

He shot me the wicked grin I adored, and he did.

EPILOGUE

Lia

A FEW MONTHS LATER...

I stood in the entrance to the living room, wondering how in the world I was ever going to break the news I had to Zeke.

Not that I didn't know that he wouldn't be angry.

But it was pretty unexpected, and I wasn't quite sure I completely absorbed the information myself.

He was on the phone, and I listened to his conversation unabashedly since he was discussing a wedding.

"Do you really think he's actually going to get married this time?" Zeke asked, sounding bemused.

He listened to whoever was on the other end of the conversation, and then he looked up, smiling broadly as he saw me step into the living room.

My heart skittered just like it always did every single time I saw my handsome husband. I was pretty sure I'd never see him shoot that grin at me without my heart speeding up.

There was no getting used to this man who loved me, and there was no way I was ever not going to feel like the luckiest woman in the world every time he looked at me like I was the most important person in the world to him.

I'd waited too long for him to be mine to ever take him for granted.

"Okay," Zeke said into his cell. "I'll let you know when he calls. And yeah, I'll be there. Hopefully Lia can come with me."

He said his good-byes and turned his phone off.

"What was that about? Is somebody getting married?"

"Yeah," he answered. "One of my friends from Harvard. That was my buddy, Barrett. He just called to let me know that we'd be getting an invitation from our mutual friend, Paul."

I hadn't met any of Zeke's old friends from Harvard since they were out of state, but I knew he maintained those relationships as often as he could. "That's good, right?" I asked because he didn't look like he was thrilled with the news.

"It will be great if he finally finds the right woman," he said thoughtfully. "Paul is kind of the male version of the Runaway Bride. He's tried this a couple of times and never went through with it. Barrett and I are hoping that he finally ties the knot."

"Are we going?" I asked as I sat next to him on the couch.

He smirked. "Up to you. It might all be for nothing. But he's doing a destination wedding somewhere tropical."

"We'll go," I said immediately. "I want you to be able to keep in touch with your friends. And I'm not going to object to going somewhere exotic and tropical with you. When is the wedding?"

"I'm not sure. But pretty soon, according to Barrett. Why? Are you planning on leaving me?" he joked.

"No," I said hesitantly. "I asked because I want to make sure I can travel. Oh, damn. I don't know exactly how to say this, Zeke."

He lifted a brow. "What? Are you okay, baby?"

"I'm pregnant," I said in a rush before I could stop myself. "I know we didn't plan this, but I know we both want to have kids someday. My body just jumped the gun. Maybe the Pill is ninety-nine percent effective, but I guess I'm the other one percent. I'm sorry."

"Don't," he said as he pulled me into his lap. "Don't ever be sorry about getting pregnant. I was there, too, and it wasn't your fault. I'm happy, sweetheart. I guess I'm just...stunned."

I wrapped my arms around him. "Me, too."

"How far along?" he asked, his voice getting more serious. "Is everything okay? Are you and the baby okay?"

"God, I love you," I said with a groan.

I should have known that Zeke's first concern would be for me and our unborn baby's health.

He rocked me like I was a child, and the motion felt so good. "Both of us are fine," I informed him. "And I'm only about a month and a half along. I get a little queasy at times, which is why I finally went and got checked out. I guess we celebrated a little too hard on your birthday."

I'd given Zeke anything and everything he'd wanted for his birthday, and almost every item had involved some kind of sex. Not that I'd had any complaints about his dirty mind.

"I think we should buy a house so we have a yard, and we need to get a room ready. Are we going to find out if it's a boy or a girl? Not that I really care, but it would be nice to know in advance—unless you want to be surprised."

I smiled at his harried expression and frantic tone. "I'm not delivering tomorrow, Zeke. We have at least seven months. And the baby isn't going to care if we live in a condo or a house. We'll figure everything out as we go along."

"Are you happy?" he questioned in an uncharacteristically vulnerable voice.

I nodded. "Very. I mean, I wouldn't have planned it this way. I'm getting ready to open another store, but we're doing so well that I can get another manager, so yeah, I'm ecstatic."

Knowing that my body was sheltering a baby that Zeke and I created with love could never be a bad thing for me. It was a miracle. And I couldn't see it any other way.

Zeke stopped rocking and just held me. I put my head on his shoulder as he said, "I'll take good care of you, sweetheart. Never feel like you're doing this alone. I love this baby already."

He put a gentle hand on my still-flat belly, and my heart almost exploded.

I put my hand on top of his and sighed.

It was going to take some time for us to get used to the fact that we were going to be parents, but very little scared me anymore.

I felt like Zeke and I had gone full circle together, and there wasn't much we couldn't handle in the future as long as we did it together.

"Are you hungry?" he asked. "You should eat."

I shifted on his lap and straddled him. "I'm not hungry for food. I'm afraid that pregnancy seems to make me crave sex and not dinner right now."

My hormones seemed to be raging, and the only thing I really thought about was getting down and dirty with my husband.

He lifted a brow. "You sure?"

I nodded, amused by his uncertainty, something that I never saw on his face. "It's perfectly safe to have as much sex as we want."

"Then I'm your man," he told me in a sexy baritone that made all of my hormones stand up and pay attention.

"Yes, you are," I said right before I leaned down and kissed him.

Zeke Conner was *always* going to be my man, and as he wrapped his arms around me, holding me protectively, I was pretty damn glad I'd gotten dumped at the altar.

It wasn't the wedding itself that had really mattered.

Happiness was all about just marrying the right guy.

~ *The End* ~

PLEASE VISIT ME AT:

http://www.authorjsscott.com
http://www.facebook.com/authorjsscott
https://www.instagram.com/authorj.s.scott
https://www.snapchat.com/add/authorjsscott

You can write to me at
jsscott_author@hotmail.com

You can also tweet
@AuthorJSScott

Subscribe to my newsletter and receive three
never before published short stories.

BOOKS BY J.S. SCOTT:

The Billionaire's Obsession Series:

The Billionaire's Obsession
Heart Of The Billionaire
The Billionaire's Salvation
The Billionaire's Game
Billionaire Undone
Billionaire Unmasked
Billionaire Untamed
Billionaire Unbound
Billionaire Undaunted
Billionaire Unknown
Billionaire Unveiled
Billionaire Unloved
Billionaire Unchallenged

The Sinclairs:

The Billionaire's Christmas
No Ordinary Billionaire
The Forbidden Billionaire
The Billionaire's Touch
The Billionaire's Voice
The Billionaire Takes All
The Billionaire's Secrets
Only A Millionaire

The Accidental Billionaires:

Ensnared

The Walker Brothers:

Release!
Player!
Damaged!

Books With Ruth Cardello:

Well Played
Well Received

A Dark Horse Novel:

Bound
Hacked

The Vampire Coalition Series:

The Vampire Coalition: The Complete Collection
Ethan's Mate
Rory's Mate
Nathan's Mate
Liam's Mate
Daric's Mate

The Sentinel Demons:

The Sentinel Demons: The Complete Collection
A Dangerous Bargain
A Dangerous Hunger
A Dangerous Fury
A Dangerous Demon King

The Curve Collection: Big Girls And Bad Boys
The Changeling Encounters Collection

Printed in Great Britain
by Amazon